I Came
to a Castle

Also available in Large Print
by Velda Johnston:

Flight to Yesterday
Face in the Shadows
Man at Windmere
White Pavilion
Girl on the Beach

I Came
to a Castle

VELDA JOHNSTON

G.K. HALL & CO.
Boston, Massachusetts
1991

Published in Large Print by arrangement with
Blassingame-Spectrum Corporation.

G.K. Hall Large Print Book Series.

Set in 18 pt. Plantin.

Library of Congress Cataloging-in-Publication Data

Johnston, Velda.
    I came to a castle / Velda Johnston.
      p. cm.—(G.K. Hall large print book series)
    ISBN 0-8161-5014-1 (lg. print)
    1. Large type books. I. Title. II. Series.
  [PS3560.O394I14 1991]
  813'.54—dc20   90-26887

To my husband, Robert G. Heslop,
without whose encouragement and aid
this book would not have been written

1

THE VAST PLAIN, tawny as a lion's skin, lay baking under the late afternoon sun. Even in the back seat of this air-conditioned car, I felt too warm. But that, I knew, was illusion, induced by the heat shimmers through which low-growing chaparral and occasional junipers seemed to dance, and by the dust cloud rising from beneath the wheels of the limousine about fifty feet ahead. Looking back through the rear window, I saw that the vehicles which followed—station wagons, flatbed trucks, and two refrigerator trucks—were also stirring up dust. I had a sudden vision of how we would appear from the air, a caravan of more than a dozen vehicles, each in its cloud of dust, crawling toward that mesa in the distance.

Beside me my two young charges, Steven and Tommy, were at the moment mercifully absorbed by the transistor radio on Steven's lap. He'd tuned in a children's program from Madrid. For a few minutes I listened idly. The announcer was extolling accomplishments during the past year of various youngsters all over the world. In Poland a fifteen-year-old chess player had competed successfully against a Grand Master. In Scotland a thirteen-year-old had sighted a new comet. In the United States, a nine-year-old Chicago girl had saved her five-year-old sister from drowning.

My attention wandered. Beyond the glass partition which separated us from the front seat, Kurt, the bull-necked chauffeur, had turned to make some smiling comment to Juanita, the housemaid who rode beside him. I saw the cool expression of her pretty profile as she made a brief reply. I hoped she'd go on being cool to him. I didn't like Kurt, and I did like Juanita. At eighteen, she was only four years younger than myself. And yet she had a simplicity, a bubbling cheerfulness, that made me think of her almost as a child.

Beyond those two in the front seat, I could see the rear window of the lead car. Max Hind, whose money and whose will had set this caravan in motion, was invisible in the left-hand corner of the rear seat. But I could see his dark-haired sister, the Contessa As-

2

coli. Her profile, sharp except for the sensuously heavy mouth, was turned toward the passenger in the right-hand corner. He too was invisible to me, but I knew he was Paul Duvall, ten years the Contessa's junior, and her lover.

I thought, "What a potpourri of nationalities!" I was American. The two orphans beside me were half-American and half-English. Kurt was German, and Juanita of Spanish peasant stock. Paul Duvall was French. The Contessa and her brother, Max Hind, were both Texas-born, but neither of them had been back to the United States for at least twenty years. Did they still consider themselves American? Perhaps. Perhaps not. Great wealth is its own nationality. And Max Hind was very rich indeed.

Steven shouted, above the sound of the radio, "I see it, I see it! I see the castle!"

His younger brother crowded past my knees to press his nose against the car window. "Where? Where?"

Steven said, with eight-year-old scorn, "On the mesa, stupid. You always build a castle on high ground."

I too could see it now, a mass of gray granite rising from the mesa at its sheer-walled northern end. The only details I could make out at this distance were flat-topped round towers, set at each of the two corners visible to me. But my heart quickened with some of the same excitement the boys' voices held. Through my mind, too, trouped the images conjured up by the word "castle"— mailed knights, dank dungeons, captive princesses—

Tommy turned to me, his blue eyes trustful. With pride, I thought of how much both boys had changed in the ten months since I'd first met them, in the Contessa's villa at San Ysidro. Then they'd faced me hostilely, almost viciously, like the well-fed, well-dressed, but otherwise neglected young animals they were.

He said, "Dinah, is it a real castle?"

"Very real. And it's been there since the eleventh century."

He frowned. "Did Uncle Max own it then?"

Steven snorted. I said swiftly, "No, dear. That was long, long before your Uncle Max was born. He bought the castle four years ago." And, I'd heard, had spent a fortune since then installing bathrooms, air conditioning, a heating plant, and an elevator to carry his crippled body up to his own suite of rooms.

"How long will we stay here?"

I said, looking at a thick stand of juniper, dark green against the base of the mesa's tawny western wall, "About three weeks or a month, according to your Aunt Julia."

Again he pressed his nose to the window. The road had curved, approaching the sloping southern end of the mesa. I could see a third round tower now, and the top of a fourth, the northeastern one. With brief puzzlement, I saw that it was not flat-topped like the others. Bulbous-roofed, it might have been part of a small mosque. I transferred my attention to the narrow windows in the castle's façade, behind which men long dead must once have stood, crossbows drawn, eyes grimly staring at attackers who swarmed, perhaps yelling, up the mesa's sloping southern end toward the outer wall. For surely once there must have been an outer wall, protecting the castle on its western and southern sides. Probably there'd been a moat, too.

"Why?" Tommy asked.

"Why what, dear?"

"Why is a castle?"

It was the sort of simple question which sets an adult floundering. After a moment I said, "Noblemen built castles to help defend land under their control. If a nobleman had to, when enemies invaded his territory, he could shut himself up in his castle and last out a siege."

As Tommy opened his mouth I added hastily, "A siege is the surrounding of your castle by your enemies. They try to starve you into surrender."

He was frowning again. Thank heaven he was a little boy. I'd have had to try to break a girl of that habit, lest she develop premature wrinkles.

"Why did Uncle Max and Aunt Julia want to come here?"

"Now there's a silly question," Steven said. "It's going to be sort of a vacation, stupid."

"I thought you promised me not to use words like silly and stupid when you talk to your brother."

"Okay." His tone strove for nonchalance, but he looked a bit shamefaced.

As a matter of fact, his little brother's question was one which had occurred to me. Why had Julia Ascoli, in torrid September, been willing to leave the cool and pretty seaside town of San Ysidro? Why had she consented to leave all her friends—all but Paul—and spend weeks in the company of her eccentric and crippled brother, her nephews, and all those servants in the vehicles which trailed this one? As far as I knew, she read nothing except the French and English and American magazines which chronicled the activities of fashionable nomads like herself. She could have no antiquarian interest in that gray pile we approached, that once-grim structure which had become a rich man's toy, bought with oil gushing from the Texas earth, an ocean and a continent's breadth away.

We were climbing the mesa's sloping southern end now. I could see the castle clearly—the rounded arch of the opening in the rough-stoned front wall, the crenelated battlements, the arrow slits in the round towers.

And I could see something else. Some five hundred feet ahead, about halfway between us and the castle, two red-painted wooden structures, like open, upended coffins, stood at either side of the road.

I stared at them.

Always I've been skeptical about extrasensory perception—perhaps because, until that moment, I'd never had reason to believe I myself possessed any such ability. And even now I can't claim that I was visited by a real premonition. In my mind's ear I heard no screams from contorted faces, no bullying shouts, no grind of ancient stone against stone. Rather, all I felt was a sudden unease—nameless, and yet so strong that I shivered. Then, aware that even in their excitement the boys might notice, I forced myself to clasp my hands in my lap and look calmly and consideringly at those narrow boxes.

They resembled guardhouses. Could they be? Oh, surely not. And yet—

A castle. Why is a castle? A castle is for refuge against besiegers.

Turning, I looked back through the rear window at all those station wagons and trucks bearing servants, and canned and frozen foods, and cases of liquor and wines, and perhaps almost every sort of necessity and luxury, from facial tissues to the sable throw for Julia Ascoli's bed.

Why all those tons of supplies when, according to the map I'd consulted the night before in my room at the Contessa's villa, there was a fairly large town only thirty miles north of here?

It seemed incredible, at this late date in the twentieth century. And yet surely it looked as if we'd come here, not for a vacation, but to withstand a siege.

2

WE DROVE BETWEEN those two upended red coffins, and past a point where a side road, little more than a dirt track, ran to the right and disappeared around the castle's southeast corner. Ahead was that rounded arch. It was the opening, I saw a moment later, of a tunnel about thirty feet long that ran through the entire southern side of the castle.

We emerged into a cobblestoned courtyard, its western side now deep in the shadow. Before the car had come to a complete stop, Steven and Tommy were fumbling at the door handles. I let them get out. No fear that they'd race excitedly to their Aunt Julia. They'd long since learned, poor mites, not to do that. Kurt opened the car door wider for me, and I made my own more sedate exit.

The castle, I saw, was built around a hollow square. I counted three stories of windows rising to the battlements. The windows here were wider than the ones in the exterior walls. After a moment I realized why. An ancient inhabitant of this place, looking out a window that faced the courtyard, would be less in danger of having an enemy arrow pierce his heart.

Looking to my left, I saw that the entire ground floor of the western side of the quadrangle had been converted into a cement-floored garage, with space for at least twenty cars. All six of the wide overhead doors had been raised. At the garage's northern end stood a gas pump, with a grease pit beside it.

I turned back, and saw that the Contessa and Paul Duvall had emerged from the other limousine. They stood on the cobblestones, quietly talking, while Kurt and the other chauffeur, a burly Spaniard named Ernesto, took a collapsible wheelchair from the car's trunk and set it up. Ernesto opened the car's rear door.

I said swiftly, "Boys, look up there. See how the tops of the walls are cut in a sort of jigsaw pattern? That's called crenelation." I was sure that Max Hind must dislike being watched during those few seconds when, helpless as a baby, he was carried from the car to his chair.

It was safe to look now. He sat with a dark

10

red blanket covering his useless legs. His hands, resting on the wheelchair's wooden arms, were wide and powerful-looking. So was the torso clad in a gray jacket of Italian slubbed silk. But the face beneath the still-thick, graying hair, with its broad forehead, its tired and yet somehow fierce eyes behind horn-rimmed glasses, and its wide, thin mouth, was the face of a scholar—an embittered scholar.

Because my father and mother had once done a magazine article on Max Hind, I knew quite a lot about him. By the age of thirty-five he'd parlayed his first oil strikes into one of the world's great fortunes, with holdings in shipping and armaments as well as oil. And at that point he'd quit. He'd simply turned over his financial affairs to a small army of managers, and quit. Not to pursue women or renown as an art collector, but knowledge. This Texas rancher's son, who'd never finished high school, had set out to transform himself into a Renaissance man, taking, if not all of knowledge for his province, at least the sciences. To that end, he'd studied for the last twenty-five years with hired teachers, all of them scholars in the field of geology, biology, chemistry, astronomy, and archaeology. He'd built a well-equipped chemistry laboratory in the dwelling where he spent most of his time, a Georgian house southwest of London. He'd financed and participated in archaeological expeditions to Central America and Asia Minor. The plane crash which he'd survived, semiparalyzed, in his forty-seventh year had only increased his determination to absorb the learning of the centuries.

But he hadn't been content to master the discoveries and theories of other men. He himself desired recognition as a brilliant theoretician. And there he'd failed, despite the journals he'd founded from time to time to disseminate his theories as to the location of lost Atlantis, or the origin of the Polynesian people, or the instinctual pattern which impels bird migration. The scientific world had merely smiled.

Now, looking at him as Ernesto wheeled him across the cobblestones, I felt a surge of pity. How galling for him, who with one phone call could shake a financial empire, to know that he was only a figure of fun to some college professor wearing a slightly frayed suit and driving a five-year-old Buick.

The trucks, which after a while would return to San Ysidro, still waited outside the courtyard, but six station wagons had driven in. Male and female members of Max Hind's staff, most of them recently hired in San Ysidro, had emerged from the vehicles and begun to unload small mountains of luggage. They were all Spanish, by the looks of them, and the women, in their blue denim skirts and blouses, appeared almost as sturdy as the men. Fascinated, I watched a tall woman—cook? housemaid?—haul a leather trunk out of a station wagon as easily as if it had been an overnight bag. Then, with a start, I turned and looked around for the Contessa. Apparently she'd gone inside.

"Come, boys," I said.

Crossing the cobblestones, we stepped into a stone-floored corridor that seemed to run the length of the castle's north side. Wrought-iron chandeliers hung from its vaulted ceiling. Directly in front of us was another doorway. As we stepped through it, I realized we must be entering what had once been the Great Hall, or main assembly room, because it was at least seventy feet long. Only its size, though, was reminiscent of the Middle Ages. Despite the confusion—luggage-laden servants hurrying past me, trucks driving into the courtyard—I got an impression of seventeenth- and eighteenth-century French furniture, and Aubusson carpets, and yellow silk draperies at wide casement windows, all blending into a suggestion of a multimillionaire's Manhattan town house or Loire Valley château.

After a moment I saw the Contessa. She sat, dark head with its postiche of false curls bent, on a small brocade sofa beside Paul. He was lighting her cigarette.

"Wait here," I said to the boys.

As I approached the two on the sofa, Paul looked up. He was a superlatively handsome man, with dark, loosely waving hair worn rather long in back, dark eyes, straight features, and a mouth with a sensuously full lower lip. Although he was around thirty-five, he appeared young enough that his informal garb—gray slacks, blue cableknit sweater with the sleeves pushed up to show his bronzed forearms—didn't seem too youthful for him. No doubt what kept him lean and hard was his devotion to sports car racing, steeple-chasing, and ski-jumping.

Such fashionable ways of courting suicide are expensive, of course. From the Contessa, who was disconcertingly frank about such matters, I'd heard that since Paul was eighteen, a series of wealthy ladies had paid his bills. For the past two years, Julia Ascoli, had enjoyed that honor. And, she'd stated to me, she intended to go on doing so as long as possible.

Paul was regarding me now with frank dislike in his dark eyes. It had been there ever since an afternoon three months before, at the San Ysidro villa. The previous day the Contessa had flown to Madrid for shopping. As I sat reading on the balcony above the small, flower-filled rear courtyard, I'd thought myself alone in the house except for the Contessa's three servants and for Steven and Tommy, whom I'd left in their room squabbling happily over a game of jack-straws.

I'd heard swift, quiet footsteps behind me, and then felt lips press the back of my neck.

Startled, I dropped the book and sprang to my feet. I turned. Paul Duvall stood there. In a striped Basque shirt, faded blue jeans, and roped espadrilles, he looked like an advertising poster for a Mediterranean resort.

I cried, "What are you doing here?" The Contessa had mentioned that he too would be away, looking at a small sloop he might buy. "I thought you were going to San Sebastian."

He smiled. "And miss an opportunity like this? Don't be silly."

I felt a surge of anger. Oh, it wasn't the

15

kiss. I'd been kissed before, and not just on the nape of the neck. It was his smiling assumption that I, as a sort of upper servant, couldn't possibly object to fun-and-games in the Contessa's absence.

"Don't ever try that again," I said coldly.

He still smiled. "Why not?"

"Because you don't appeal to me." That happened to be true. To appeal to me, men have to be men. And I can't shake off the notion that a man who trades on his looks, however virile they may be, is somehow effeminate.

He flushed beneath his deep tan. After a moment he said, "And now I suppose you'll run to Julia." He'd spoken mockingly, but his eyes were uneasy.

"No, I don't consider the matter that important." That wasn't my real reason. My real reason was that if I talked, Paul wouldn't be the one she'd fire. I'd be.

Evidently he'd had time to realize that too, because he said coldly, "Smart girl. You wouldn't be doing yourself any good, you know." Turning, he walked toward the outside staircase which descended from one end of the balcony.

He'd returned his gaze to Julia Ascoli

now. I stopped in front of her and said, "Contessa?"

Turning her head, she looked up at me vaguely. "Yes?"

Hers wasn't a vicious face. But then, as I'd discovered over the past ten months, she wasn't a vicious woman. She was merely as self-centered as an infant. And she was lazy. If she hadn't been able to hire people to draw her baths, dress her, groom her, and pound and massage her body into shape, she probably would have been one of the frumpiest women alive.

"Our rooms," I said. "The boys and mine. Where are they?"

"What? Oh. My brother said there was a chart." She gestured with the hand that held her cigarette. "In the corridor, near where you came in."

I thanked her, and started away. She said, "Miss Haversham."

I turned back. "Yes, Contessa?"

"You and the boys will take your meals in your rooms. Juanita will serve them to you. But you can use the library, and you can walk out onto the mesa if you like."

She meant that everywhere else was off limits to us. She hadn't sounded cold as she

17

said it, but neither had she seemed the least apologetic. "Very well, Contessa."

Rejoining the boys, I went out into the corridor with them. On the bare stone wall, just to the right of the entrance from the courtyard, hung a chart showing the castle's floor plan. But not the complete plan, I realized instantly. The whole eastern side of the four-sided structure had been omitted. That must mean, I decided, that those rooms were to be occupied by the Contessa and her brother and Paul Duvall, together with their personal servants. What's more, there was no chart of the third floor or the round towers. Why? Because those areas were unused, or used solely for storage? Probably.

The boys, restless now, had begun to tug at my hands, but I went on studying the chart for a minute or so. The south side of the quadrangle, on the opposite side of the courtyard, housed on its ground floor the kitchen, bakeroom, laundry, supply rooms, repair shop, and one room labeled, mysteriously, "su." The rooms above were all labeled either "s," or "s-s," which must mean they were to be occupied by servants, sometimes two to a room. Probably Max Hind's housekeeper, a Scotswoman who'd accompanied him from his English estate, would assign those rooms.

Some of the rooms on the second floor of the western side, above that long garage, were labeled "s," but most of them were blank. As for the side in which I stood, the ground floor—from west to east—housed the library, that huge drawing room I'd just left, a dining room somewhat smaller, a billiard room, and a gun room.

It was on the plan for the second floor of this side of the quadrangle that I found the room assigned to me, although not by name. The first two rooms at the western end were blank, the third was assigned to Steven and Thomas Marsden, and the fourth was labeled "governess." After that there was a blank square, and then a room labeled "s." Probably, I decided, that would be occupied by Juanita.

According to the chart, the way to get to our rooms was by stairs somewhere to my right. "I've found our rooms. Come, Steven, Tommy."

At the end of the corridor we walked through an archway and found the stairs—and were instantly far back in the Middle Ages. They were steep, and claustrophobically narrow, each step worn to a hollow in the middle by feet of men and women who'd died centuries ago. I started climbing, followed by the children.

Halfway up Steven shouted, his voice ringing in that confined space, "I want to look at that big room down there!"

I turned. He was plunging down the stairs, with his younger brother close behind him. "Boys! The Contessa—"

"She won't be there," Steven flung over his shoulder. At the foot of the stairs both children turned and disappeared through the archway.

I felt chagrin. For many months now, they'd been so obedient, so eager to please. But after all, even the best-behaved small boys, finding themselves in a place like this, couldn't be expected to remain quietly on the leash.

I followed them down the stairs and back along the corridor. When I reached the drawing room I saw with relief that Steven had been right. The little brocade sofa was empty. Apparently the Contessa and Paul, satisfied that enough luggage had been carried in to insure their creature comforts, had retired to their own quarters. Now the huge room was empty except for a manservant, straightening rugs which the luggage-laden men and women had rumpled, and my two young charges, staring at a tall glass curio cabinet filled with jade figurines. "Boys!" I called.

They looked at me. "We want to see what's in there!" Steven shouted. With Tommy close behind him, he raced toward a doorway about thirty feet to my left. I followed, threading my way past sofas and armchairs and little gilt tables, and passed through a wide doorway into the next room. Steven and Tommy stood on the far side of a massive refectory table, snapping open and shut the lids of a twin-welled bronze ink-stand. Steven greeted me with the disgusted comment, "Nothing but books."

He was almost right. The room did contain a card catalogue cabinet, several straight-backed chairs, and two black leather armchairs. But it was books which dominated the big room. Mostly in leather bindings, which appeared to range in age from a couple of centuries to almost new, they lined all four walls from parquet floor to lofty ceiling. Only a massive fireplace, with some sort of chart hanging above it, broke that solid expanse of tooled leather. What's more, apparently they'd been arranged according to an index, rather than just for appearance's sake, because tall and heavy books stood side-by-side with pocket-sized ones. Moving close to the north side of the room, I saw I was right. Each book spine bore a number. With awe I reflected that this room must hold as many books as the small public library in Twin Hills, North Dakota.

Turning, I saw that the boys had disappeared. I hurried back into the drawing room just in time to see Tommy open the doors of a bay-fronted rosewood cabinet. Bending slightly, he peered in at the multicolored bottles of brandy, vodka, Scotch, and liqueurs.

I said, in my enough-of-this-nonsense voice, "Close that! And come with me."

They trotted meekly to me. This time, when we reached the staircase, I herded them ahead of me up the worn stone steps. We emerged onto the landing, with a stone-floored corridor stretching away to the right. To the left, set in an embrasure in the thick wall, was a narrow casement window, slightly opened. Curious, I stepped into the embrasure and pushed the windowpanes farther apart.

Directly below, at the foot of the castle's steep western wall, someone had caused yellow marigolds and pink zinnias to spring from the arid earth. They grew on all four sides of a rectangular area, paved with white flagstones, and set with a table and chairs of lacy ironwork, painted white. From the table's center rose a fringed umbrella, now furled.

My gaze traveled out over the mesa, dotted with juniper and gray-green clumps of chaparral, to the point where it dropped sharply away. Beyond I could see a stretch of open plain, and then the blue dazzle of the sea, perhaps fifty miles away. Recalling that the sea had been invisible from below the mesa, and even from part way up its sloping southern end, I realized that I must be standing at least two hundred feet above the plain.

Steven tugged at my arm. "I want to see."

He was tall enough to peer over the window ledge, but when it was Tommy's turn I had to boost him up and hold him there. "See that streak of blue? That's the ocean."

"Where San Ysidro is?"

"Oh, no, dear! San Ysidro's away to the south, on the Mediterranean. That's the Atlantic Ocean out there."

I lowered him to the floor. As we turned away from the embrasure, I saw that to my left a second flight of ancient stairs, just as worn as those we'd climbed, rose steeply toward the third floor. We walked down the corridor, with its row of closed doors on one side, and on the other the castle's outer wall, set with windows only about fifteen inches wide. Those windows in the drawing room, I decided, must originally have been no wider.

When we reached the third door, I opened it. Yes, this was Steven and Tommy's room.

Steven took several steps inside, and then halted. "For cripe's sake," he said in his most scornfully sophisticated tone.

I could understand his reaction. Oh, the room was large enough—at least fifteen feet by eighteen—to accommodate their elaborate electric train set. The shaggy brown carpet appeared to be of appropriate sturdiness. The small beds, placed on opposite sides of the room, looked almost like duplicates of the ones they'd slept in at the villa. The wall shelves looked adequate for all the toys which would be unloaded from one of those trucks down there.

It was the wallpaper which had evoked Steven's disdain. On it a cowboy, duplicated over and over again, rode a mustang in pursuit of a similarly duplicated steer. What minion, acting on orders filtered down through upper servants to prepare this room for small boys, had chosen that wallpaper?

"The walls ought to be stone," my little purist said. "Do they think this is a ranch, for cripe's sake?"

"Never mind. They're stone underneath the paper." And under a coat of plaster too, undoubtedly. "Anyway, you can always look down into the courtyard. That way you'll be sure it's still a castle." As they both rushed toward the window, I called to Steven, "And don't say 'for cripe's sake.' "

A door in the left-hand wall stood partly open. I went through it and found myself in a small but adequate bathroom, with yellow fixtures and brown tiled walls. A second door led to what was undoubtedly my room.

It was smaller, I found, than the boys' room. Evidently the space for the bath's installation had been subtracted from it. But it was pleasant enough, with its black walnut furniture and floral-patterned rug. On the left side of the casement window an air-conditioning unit projected from the wall. I touched a switch, and heard a low hum. Then cool air rippled against my face and through my hair.

The boys were clattering across the bath

into my room. Turning, I saw their doleful faces. "No TV," Steven announced.

"It's probably down on one of the trucks."

"No, they left it behind. And there's no TV downstairs, either. And no radio."

"Maybe they're set in a wall, behind screens." In Julia Ascoli's jewel box of a drawing room at the villa, doors covered with yellow silk had concealed wall installations of TV and stereo.

"Tommy and I looked, and we didn't see anything like that."

"Well, I'll ask about getting you a set. By the way, where's your radio? Did you leave it in the car?"

They looked at each other, and then nodded.

"No telling where it's been taken," I said. "I don't want to bother anyone about it now. Tomorrow I'll run it down for you."

"No TV," Tommy mourned. "No little radio."

I turned back to the air conditioner. Frowning, I switched it off. It seemed to me that there was something else missing in this ancient structure, its thick walls now honeycombed with the miles of pipes and conduits necessary for modern bathrooms, and air conditioning, and an elevator. It was something one expects to find in all but the humblest dwellings.

I had it. Neither in the drawing room, nor the library, nor the corridors, nor the boys' room, nor my own, had I seen any sign of a telephone.

3

SOMEONE KNOCKED. I opened my door to find a burly, sweating man, one of the servants hired in San Ysidro, standing there with four pieces of luggage. Each big hand grasped a dark blue suitcase. The two other bags, brown leather ones, he'd managed to wedge between his sides and his brawny arms.

I said in Spanish, "The blue cases are mine. The others belong next door."

He took a step into the room, placed my suitcases on the floor, and let the other two slide down his body until he could catch the handles. A moment or so after he returned to the corridor, I heard the door of the next room open and close.

I turned to the boys. "Would you like to play jackstraws?" Aware that some time might pass before they received their big chest of toys, which I'd seen loaded onto a truck rather than into a station wagon, I'd tucked the jackstraw set into one of my suit-cases.

"With you?" Tommy asked. He loved to play against me, because quite often I lost to him, and not always by design. Steven never lost to either of us.

"No, I have things to do." I didn't, really. Unpacking my sparse belongings would take only a few minutes. But I wanted to be alone with my puzzled thoughts.

"Aren't we going to explore?" Steven asked.

"Later." No point in telling them how limited our explorations would be. Perhaps I could get that rule relaxed somewhat.

When I'd settled them in their room with the jackstraws, I returned to my own room. Standing at the window, I looked down be-tween its casement panes of leaded glass at the courtyard below. Men and a few women were still unloading the trucks. Most of the crates and barrels were being carried into what in medieval times were called the "offices"—the southern or service side of the quadrangle. As I watched, a man ex-tracted a whole side of beef from a refrigeration truck and, slightly bent under its weight, carried it across the cobblestones.

I was about to turn away from the window when I saw the Contessa and Paul Duvall. Seemingly oblivious of the bustle all around them, they strolled across the courtyard. As I watched them enter the shadowy tunnel beneath the castle's southern side, I thought of the first day I heard Julia Ascoli's voice.

It had been raining in Paris that December afternoon. I'd sat in the sidewalk portion of the Brasserie Lipp, staring at a dead leaf which had plastered itself against the glass enclosure. On the round table beside me rested a coffee cup and the Paris *Tribune*.

I'd bought the paper a few minutes before at the downstairs newspaper stand of Le Drugstore, a few doors away along the Boulevard St. Germaine. Carefully I'd avoided looking at the magazine racks, which held everything from *Playboy* to *Réalités*, and from *Punch* to *Paris-Match*. Too many of those magazines, especially the American ones, had at one time or another carried my father's articles, and my mother's sensitive photographs.

As I sat staring at that dead leaf, I knew that I should be in my room on the Avenue de la Reine, studying the plays of Racine for my next examination at the Sorbonne. But did I care that much about obtaining my Master's degree in French literature? Did I care that much about anything? At the moment, I didn't. I was still sunk deep in the apathy that had followed the first shock, two months before, of my parents' death.

And yet I was not quite twenty-two. That meant I had years and years to spend in one fashion or another. The question was, what fashion? I could go on with my studies, although studying came hard these days, and obtain my Master's, and teach almost anywhere I liked. My parents had banked money for my Sorbonne expenses before starting out on their last and fatal assignment. Eventually I'd have money from their estate. Not much—journalists seldom get rich—but perhaps enough to see me through until I found a job.

Or I could go back to Two Hills, North Dakota, where I'd spent the first nine years of my life, and where my grandparents still lived. Or I could marry the young Englishman who for six months had been asking me to. He was studying at the Sorbonne for his Doctorate in musicology. He was the son of a Harley Street surgeon, reasonably good-looking, and thoroughly nice. The only thing wrong with him was that I didn't love him.

And so where did that leave me?

On impulse I picked up the *Tribune*. Ignoring the headlines, which dealt with the Middle Eastern conflict, I turned to the classified ads. Always they'd fascinated me, what with their job offers to persons wishing to join expeditions up the Amazon, and their job-seeking "cultured and personable" young men, willing to do "anything legal."

Halfway down Employment Opportunities, Female, I saw the ad:

"Governess wanted for boys, aged eight and five, in Mediterranean resort. Must be English-speaking, and in twenties. Excellent salary, pleasant room. Reverse charges." There was a name, Ascoli, and a telephone number.

Raising my eyes, I looked at that dead leaf, and the rain-drenched pedestrians beyond it hurrying through the gray light. In that Mediterranean resort, wherever it was, there'd be blessed sunlight, and a beach of fine white sand, and a sparkling, million-faceted sea.

Looking back at the ad, I reread the words "pleasant room." I thought of my own cramped room in that Left Bank hotel, with its bath down the hall.

"Reverse charges." It would cost me nothing to call.

Leaving money beside my saucer, I hurried back through winding and narrow streets to my hotel. In the small lobby Madame Berthot, the middle-aged and faintly mustached manageress, sat behind the battered reception desk. We exchanged nods. I walked past her to the tiny telephone booth, gave the international operator the number and the name Ascoli, and asked her to reverse charges. She told me she'd call back.

No point in waiting in that confined space. I went out into the lobby and sat down in a plastic chair with aluminum arms. "I've put through a long distance call. It may take time."

"But yes." Like most Parisians, she accepted the vagaries of the French telephone system just as she accepted the winter drizzle, and the *clochards* sleeping on subway gratings.

I waited almost fifteen minutes. It was long enough for me to review the folly of what I contemplated. Up until two months ago, I'd been doing fairly well in my graduate studies. And although the Sorbonne's classes were overcrowded, its library facilities inadequate, and many of its professors unapproachably aloof, conditions were still much better, everyone said, than before the student riots of a few years before. If I continued my courses there, I'd be eligible for well-paying jobs for the rest of my life.

But these past weeks I'd found it hard, agonizingly hard, to study. It might well be that I'd fail at least one of my courses. Wouldn't it be better to withdraw now, and then re-enter the university when I felt up to it?

But that, I knew, was all rationalization. The truth was that Paris, once to me as to many others the most beautiful of cities, had become the hideous place where I'd received that cablegram. I couldn't stand it here any longer, I just couldn't.

The phone rang. I went to it. "Your call is complete," the operator said, and a moment later a feminine voice said in heavily accented English, "The Contessa Ascoli's residence."

"I'm calling about the advertisement in—"

"Here is the Contessa."

Then another voice said, "Julia Ascoli speaking."

Julia Ascoli. Where had I heard that name? Oh, yes. Dad and Mother's article of three years ago on the eccentric multi-millionaire Max Hind. His sister, Julia, was the widow of a Count Ascoli.

But I mustn't remind her of that article. Not that it had been snide. My father was never snide. But the article had recounted Max Hind's misadventures in the scientific world.

"Hello? Hello?" the voice at the other end of the wire said.

"Forgive me, Contessa. I—dropped my purse." Speaking swiftly, I went on, "I think I may be qualified for the position you advertised. I'm an American, almost twenty-two years old. I speak good French, fair Spanish, and a little Italian. I've been studying at the Sorbonne for my Master's—"

"The Sorbonne!" Her voice was suspicious. "And you want to be a governess?"

I saw that, even before we met, I'd have to speak of my private agony. "I feel I can't stay here in Paris. You see, I lost my parents two months ago—"

"Both of them?"

Her question didn't strike me as brutal. Just uncaringly tactless.

"Yes." I swallowed to ease the pressure

in my throat. "They were journalists." A slip. But maybe it wouldn't matter. Anyway, it was too late now. "They were aboard a small schooner in the Caribbean, doing research for an article on the sailing ship trade between the islands. A white squall came up—"

"A what?"

"A white squall. It's a strong wind that seems to come out of nowhere in fair weather. The schooner capsized. Two men were eventually picked up alive. But the others aboard—drowned."

I had to stop. My imagination, always too graphic, had conjured up my mother, struggling in a wind-tossed sea, her light brown hair, almost the same shade as my own, plastered back from her terrified face. I saw my father, shouting her name, fighting the waves to reach her. Surely he had. It was a comfort to think that when they'd gone down, they'd been in each other's arms.

"I'm sorry," the Contessa said. Then briskly: "About the job. Tomorrow's Saturday. If I wire you the money, could you fly down here then?"

"Yes." If I changed my mind, or if she didn't want me, I could fly back in time for Monday's classes. "But where is here?"

"What? Oh. San Ysidro. Do you know it?"

"I've seen it." When I was twelve, I'd driven through the little resort, once a fishing village, on the way to Gibraltar with my parents.

"It's settled, then. If we suit each other, fine. If we don't, there'll be no harm done."

"Yes, and thank you. Goodbye, Contessa." I wanted to get out of that booth. In my thoughts a gale wind still howled, and two doomed people, locked in an embrace, looked into each other's faces for the last time.

"Wait a minute. What's your name? And where shall I send the money?"

"Oh! I'm Dinah Haversham." I added the name and address of my hotel.

We hung up, and I left the booth. As I climbed the shabbily carpeted stairs to my second floor room, I wondered who the boys mentioned in the advertisement were. The Contessa's sons? It was biologically possible, perhaps, but socially improbable. Count Ascoli had been dead for at least ten years. And since she still retained her title, his widow apparently hadn't remarried.

The money arrived early that evening. By eight the next morning I was aboard a southbound plane. Shortly before noon, I alighted from a taxi in front of a two-story white stucco villa. Grateful for the sunlight on my face and arms, I went through the gate in the low white stucco wall, and up a flag-stoned walk bordered by pink azaleas.

A large, dignified woman, apparently Spanish, admitted me to a cool hallway. From her voice I knew she was the one who'd answered the phone the day before. "I'm the housekeeper. The Contessa is in the morning room."

I followed her down the hall. At an open door she said, "Miss Haversham," and then moved on.

I entered, halting just inside the doorway. Sunlight flooded the long room through a half dozen long windows. The air was fragrant with green, growing things set in lusterware pots and jardinieres. Flowered cretonne had been used to slipcover the furniture, including a chaise longue. On it lay a brunette woman, about forty-five years old and about ten pounds overweight. She held a copy of the Paris edition of *Vogue* in her hands. On the low round table beside her was an open box of marzipan.

She smiled slightly, swung her sandaled

feet and tanned, somewhat sturdy legs to the floor, and stood up.

"Hello, Miss Haversham. I'm Julia Ascoli. Well," she said, gesturing toward two armchairs placed facing each other, "shall we sit here while we talk?" From the way she said it, I guessed that several times in the past those armchairs had held her and some prospective governess.

We sat down. Her rather prominent brown eyes studied me—not with calculated rudeness, I felt, but just with indifference as to whether or not I minded her scrutiny. I got the impression that she approved of what she saw. I could imagine her thinking, "Pretty, but not too pretty. Well dressed, but not really chic."

Or perhaps that was just my own estimation of myself. From where I sat I could see my reflection in a smoked glass mirror between two of the long windows. My light brown hair framed even but otherwise not remarkable features. My figure, a little below average height, was slender enough. My black and white checked suit of lightweight wool looked well bred, but obviously hadn't been designed by Dior.

She said, "First of all you'll want to know something about the boys. They're my nephews, or rather, half nephews. Their mother was my half sister. Their last name is Marsden. Steven is eight, and Thomas almost six."

"Their parents?"

"Both dead. Their father—he was an Englishman—died in a fire that destroyed their house in Kent four years ago. My sister died two years ago. Pneumonia. The kind penicillin can't help."

I felt disconcerted. Her tone was so matter of fact, so almost bored, that I didn't even murmur the conventional, "I'm sorry."

She said, as if sensing my reaction, "I'll be frank with you." She said it with the pride some people take in frankness, apparently feeling that it more than compensates for their lack of such virtues as patience, generosity, and tact. "I never felt close to my sister. After all, she was only a half sister— the daughter of my father's second wife— and much younger than I. She grew up in Texas. I never even saw her until she was fifteen."

I recalled then that according to my father's article Julia Ascoli too had been born on a small Texas ranch—and only a chicken ranch, at that. I could hear it, now, beneath that blended, indefinable accent which much traveled people acquire—a slight but unmistakable Texas drawl.

"And I'll be frank about something else. I've never liked being around children. I never know what to say to them. If I had my way, these two would be in school someplace, where they'd be better off. But when my sister was dying, she made my brother and me promise not to put either of them in boarding school before the age of ten. And my brother insists we have to keep the promise—although I notice," she said with faint waspishness, "that he hasn't taken them to live with him in England."

After a moment she went on, "Anyway, I doubt that any school would keep them long. I think there's something wrong with them, I really do. The younger one perhaps isn't so bad. Their last governess told me he could read a little. But Steven, who's more than two years older, can't read at all."

"What would you want me to teach them?"

She waved a hand. "Oh, whatever's customary. The main thing is to—supervise them."

Translation: Keep them out of my hair.

"No other governess has stayed more than a few months. Finally I decided that someone young and attractive might have better luck with them. You seem just the sort of person I'd hoped to find."

I murmured something appreciative.

"Except for your seeing the boys, the only thing left is the matter of salary." She mentioned a figure almost three times the monthly sum I'd been drawing from my parents' bank in Paris.

There must be something very wrong indeed with her nephews. What did they do to their governesses? Set fire to their beds?

Rising, she grasped a bell pull that hung between two of the long windows. "I'll have the boys brought in."

After less than a minute, the housekeeper appeared in the doorway. "We're ready to see the boys now, Rosa."

While we waited, Julia Ascoli asked me what the weather had been like in Paris, and how I'd enjoyed the flight down. The abstracted look in her eyes told me that she wasn't interested in the answers. Obviously she wanted to get back to her chaise, her magazine, and her marzipan.

The housekeeper brought two little boys into the room. They stood, spines stiff, a few steps inside the doorway. After a swift glance at me, both of them fastened blue eyes at some point in the air above me. They were small for their ages. The blond hair of the older boy had begun to darken, but the younger was almost a towhead. The air of this until-now pleasant room seemed to vibrate with their sullen enmity.

"Steven, Thomas, this is Miss Haversham, your new governess."

The two pairs of eyes remained fixed upon that invisible point in the air. Julia Ascoli looked at me and shrugged. "Rosa will show you the boys' room. Yours adjoins it. When you've made up your mind about my offer, let me know."

Herding the boys before her, Rosa led me down the hall and up the graceful curve of a staircase. On the upper floor she opened the door of a big, sun-flooded room, and then excused herself. The boys marched inside, the little one's shoulder almost touching the other's upper arm, to a spot about midway between the door and the long French windows opening onto a balcony. There they turned and looked at me. No, looked isn't the word. They glared. If it hadn't been so sad, the contrast between their defiance and their helpless frailty would have seemed funny.

I let my gaze wander around the room.

Besides the beds and bureaus, it contained a small fortune in toys. A carousel, equipped with four prancing steeds big enough for them to ride, and, no doubt, with a music box inside its mirrored central pillar. An elaborate electric train system, occupying about ten square feet of floor space. Here were children who had everything, except what they needed.

I smiled at them. Their expressions didn't change. "I know you don't like me. I'll bet you don't like anyone, except each other. But I like you already, and you're going to like me. I promise you that."

I walked toward them. They stiffened, but held their ground. "In the first place, my name isn't Miss Haversham. It's Dinah." I looked down into the younger boy's hostile eyes. "And I'm going to call you Tommy."

Something came into his face. Confused recollection? Pain? He looked down at the floor. I asked, "Did anyone else ever call you Tommy?"

After a moment he whispered, "I think so."

Very carefully I laid my hand on that pale, silky head. He didn't respond in any way. But neither did he draw his head from under my hand.

I looked at Steven. The child's mouth was thin with scorn. In his eyes, though, I could read the terrible fear of his brother's defection. I said, "I shan't call you Stevie. Steven is such a dignified name, just right for the head of a family. And that's what you'll be when you grow up, since you're the older brother."

He didn't speak, but his chin lifted, almost imperceptibly.

Flattery, I thought, will get me someplace.

Now, as I looked down at the courtyard, I realized that in the next room Tommy must have spilled his jackstraws, because I heard his chagrined "Aw-w-w!"

In a very real sense, those boys in there were my creation. Nobody but Juanita, the Contessa's little housemaid, had bothered to notice, but they even looked different, their faces fuller, their mouths no longer pinched, their eyes bright with small boy mischief rather than tormented hostility.

If only for their sake, I had to try to dispel the unease which, assailing me before we'd even driven into the courtyard of this place, still lingered within me.

4

CROSSING THE BATH'S tiled floor, I entered the boys' room.

"I'm going downstairs for a few minutes. Will you promise me to stay right here and go on with your game?"

Steven said, "We're tired of jackstraws."

"I put that pirate book in my suitcase. Would you like to read to your brother?"

Quickly he nodded.

As I returned to my room and took the brightly jacketed book from my suitcase, I thought with amusement of how, my third day at the San Ysidro villa, I'd discovered that Steven could not only read; he read very well indeed for an eight-year-old. He'd merely been determined, until then, not to let any adult know that he could.

A minute or so later I closed my door on the sound of his voice, reading aloud the exploits of Henry Morgan, and then paused in the stone-flagged corridor. I consulted my watch. Five-twenty. Surely Juanita wouldn't bring our supper until about six. Perhaps I'd have time to find the Contessa. Not that she'd be willing to answer my questions now, when she was in the company of Paul Duvall. But perhaps she'd tell me when she could talk with me.

As I moved toward the ancient stairwell, I reflected that, without becoming Julia Ascoli's friend, I'd become her confidante. Most nights at the villa she'd either entertained guests, or gone out somewhere. But quite often she was attacked by headaches of almost migraine severity. Scarcely one to linger beside a sick bed, Paul would vanish from her room and the villa. Then she'd summon me.

Perhaps she'd always feared her reminiscences might bore her friends. Anyway, she'd lie there in her big round bed and, her voice a little slurred with the analgesics she'd taken, talk with almost incredible frankness of her late husband, her lovers, her travels, and sometimes her childhood.

I'd been there less than a month when she said one night, "Your father was right about my parents' being poor. His *Life* article didn't say how poor, though. We had an outhouse." She laughed. "With a Sears Roebuck catalogue hanging from a nail."

I said uncomfortably, "Then you've known all along I was Joe and Diane Haversham's daughter?"

"Of course. I remember your father's article very well. And a few weeks before you phoned me I'd heard that he and his wife had drowned. And so when you said your parents were journalists, and told me what had happened to them—"

Her voice trailed off. I asked, "And you didn't mind?"

"Why should I? He didn't say anything that wasn't true about my brother, or me either.

"Damn fool," she added, and for a startled moment I thought she meant me. "Here he has all the money in the world, or most of it. And he's miserable because a lot of stoop-shouldered professors don't think he's Einstein. Why doesn't he just enjoy being rich? I have, ever since he made his first oil strike. I was eleven then. One of the first things he did was fly me to Switzerland and enroll me in a girls' school there."

She laughed. "I was the only American in my form, and I had all those English Honorables and Middle Eastern princesses and Greek shipping tycoons' daughters eating out of my hand. I told them about Texas by the hour. Some of it was true, but most of it was things I'd seen in the movies. They'd swallow anything. They even believed that when I was nine I'd helped hold off an Indian raid."

Some evenings when she summoned me to her room, she asked me about my own past life. I'd tell her of how, when I was nine, my smalltown-newspaperman father and my mother, a photographer, had taken me from North Dakota to New York. I'd tell her, too, of the years after my parents became a writer-photographer team, contributing articles, mostly on European subjects, to magazines. Whenever it wouldn't interfere with my education, they'd take me with them on their travels.

The Contessa would seem to enjoy my talk for a while, especially when I told of my grandfather, a smalltown lawyer so stubborn that he'd once carried a simple trespassing case all the way to the Supreme Court—and won. But after a while her prominent brown eyes would glaze with boredom. I'd fall silent, and she'd begin to talk.

Most often, she talked about Paul. "I know he must strike someone like you as utterly no good." Her voice reflected her amusement at such a point of view. "And he's even worse than a lot of people realize. I know he stole an emerald necklace out of old Mrs. Dalworth-Martin's bedroom safe five years ago. He thought she'd be too embarrassed to go to the police, but when he saw she wasn't, he gave the emeralds back. And I suspect he's been mixed up in a lot of things that not even I know about. But why should I mind, when he's exactly what I want?"

Now, in pursuit of her and Paul Duvall, I hurried out of the first floor corridor and across the cobblestoned courtyard. Men were still unloading one truck, but the others, apparently, had been emptied. Their drivers, waiting to start the return trip to San Ysidro, lounged against the trucks' sides, smoking slender brown cigarettes and talking quietly among themselves.

As I entered the shadowy tunnel beneath the southern side of the castle, I noticed for the first time the massive, iron-sheathed double door, each half swung back against a side of the tunnel. Probably once there'd been an even more ancient portcullis here, its toothed iron jaws ready to clang shut at the approach of an enemy. This massive door, though, at least a foot thick, looked strong enough to splinter any battering ram. As I neared the outer end of the tunnel, I saw a second and equally thick iron-sheathed door, also with each half swung back against the rough stone wall.

I stepped out onto the road. I saw no sign of the Contessa and Paul, but I did see something else—something that made me stop short in my tracks.

About a hundred yards away, three men were erecting a cross-barred gate between those two red, upended coffins.

So they *were* guardhouses.

Why guardhouses, when those massive doors back there surely could bar any intrusion? Against what possible invader could Max Hind be preparing to defend himself?

This passed beyond eccentricity. This seemed almost—paranoid. It was disturbing to realize that the two little boys in my care were now a part of this man's household.

I thought, aware of my anxiety-quickened pulse, "I've got to talk to his sister." She and Paul were nowhere in sight on the mesa, now a dull rose color under the almost level rays of the sun. That meant, probably, that they'd strolled around to that flower-bordered terrace I'd seen from a second-floor window.

Turning, I took a few hurried steps. Then again I stopped short. I'd suddenly remembered something—her voice and Paul's, rousing me from sleep one night more than a week ago.

They'd been moving along the second floor balcony that ran the entire length of the villa's rear wall. Under pressure of anger, Julia Ascoli's voice always grew loud. It was loud then.

"—bury myself in that ghastly place," I heard her say.

"It will be only a few weeks," Paul's voice answered. Then brightly, but with an undertone of anxiety, "Humor him. What is it you Americans say? Remember which side your bread is buttered on, darling."

"But there'll be no one there, absolutely no one."

"I'll be there."

"You bet you will! I told him that if you couldn't come along, I wouldn't stir a step."

"Be happy about it, darling. I am. I'll have you all to myself—"

Their voices and footsteps ceased. After perhaps a minute, I heard them moving back to the Contessa's room.

The next morning she'd informed me that Max Hind was flying down from London. "In about a week we're going up to Castle Estillio. He owns it, you know. We'll take Juanita with us. The rest of the staff stays

51

here. My brother's bringing his own people with him, and will hire others here in San Ysidro."

My heart had quickened at the news. I'd read of Castle Estillio, one of the smallest and oldest of European castles. But recalling her angry tone during that conversation on the balcony the night before, I tried not to show my pleasure at the prospect.

Now I was realizing something else about that post-midnight conversation. Paul Duvall, ordinarily the most easily bored of men, hadn't sounded just resigned at the prospect of spending weeks in this austere and lonely place. He'd seemed eagerly persuasive, even frightened lest she refuse to "humor" her brother.

Whatever Max Hind's motives, rational or irrational, in bringing us here, Paul had his own reasons for wanting to come along.

Even before Julia Ascoli had told me about old Mrs. Dalworth-Martin's emeralds, I'd sensed that underneath his surface charm, Paul was coldly corrupt. I'd been contemptuous of him, but never wary. Now, though, I felt wary, at least enough so that, while Julia Ascoli was with him, I wouldn't ask her for a future interview. Instead, I'd send her a note by Juanita.

Turning back, I hurried toward the castle's entrance.

5

BY THE TIME I'd begun to climb those narrow stairs, my alarm had abated somewhat. After all, I'd reflected, the very rich often display an exaggerated love of privacy, and a perhaps justified suspicion of the world at large, which in ordinary men might be considered paranoid. What of that legendary aviation tycoon, for instance, insisting that business colleagues confer with him at two in the morning, in the back seat of a car parked on a dark country side road?

Entering the boys' room, I found them still engrossed in the sacking of Old Panama. I crossed to my own room and unpacked my bags. I'd been about to place my suitcases in the closet when someone knocked.

I found Juanita standing in the corridor, with our dinner tray resting beside her on the flagstones. On the journey from San Ysidro she'd worn her heavy braids wrapped around her head, topped off with a black straw pillbox that she'd obtained heaven knew where. Surely it had never been part of the Contessa's wardrobe. But now a braid hung dark and lustrous over each shoulder of her blue cotton blouse.

I looked down at the tray. It was of teakwood, and laden with china, silver, a large ironware covered casserole, and napery—surely a heavy burden for a slender eighteen-year-old to carry along stone corridors and up that steep staircase. But down at the villa I'd noticed that no matter how hard she worked, she seldom lost her dimpled smile. Her dimples were showing now.

"Miss, will dine you and the boys in this room?" She was proud of her English, which had improved under my informal coaching. But she still often reversed word orders.

"No, the table's in the boys' room. I'll go around and open the door for you."

While she and I set the table, she kept up an excited chatter. Was not the castle wonderful? So many rooms! And was it not wonderful that she could go to see her mother and her sister on her free day? To think, not for two years had she seen her family.

I felt apprehensive. It was I who'd given her hope of visiting her family. The day after I'd learned we were to come to Castle Estillio, I'd looked up its location in a guidebook bought at the newsstand in San Ysidro's pretty little square. Scanning the fold-out map, I'd seen that Juanita's native village, Las Piedras, was only fifteen miles away. That night I'd told her so.

But if Max Hind had taken such extreme measures to guard the castle's privacy, wasn't it likely he'd be determined not to allow his employees to wander, gossiping, over the countryside? I said hesitantly, "I'm not sure that Mr. Hind will allow anyone to drive you there."

For a moment alarm clouded her pretty face. Then she smiled. "I will walk."

"Fifteen miles? There and back?"

"If I start before—dusk?"

"I think you mean daylight."

"If I start before daylight, I can."

She finished with the table. As she turned toward the door, the tray in her hand, I said, "Oh, one moment, please. Could you take a note to the Contessa?"

"I am sorry. I can not go to that side of this place. Señora Douglas to us gave the orders."

Mrs. Douglas was the housekeeper Max Hind had brought with him from England. "You mean that side?" I pointed to the east, and she nodded. I went on incredulously,

"You mean none of the servants is allowed in the family side of the castle?"

"Oh, some." She named the privileged few. Mrs. Douglas, of course. Kurt and Ernesto, the two burly drivers whom, I suspected, Max Hind also thought of as bodyguards. Miss Walmsey, the tall and broad-shouldered English R.N. who, ever since Max Hind's plane crash, had accompanied him almost everywhere. Griffith, his English valet. Elena, the Contessa's personal maid—

Juanita brightened. "Elena will try to take meals with us." She giggled. "Elena likes two of the men the Señor hired in San Ysidro. I will give her the note."

Hurrying into my room, I took notepaper from a bureau drawer and wrote:

Dear Contessa,
    May I talk with you for a few minutes? It's most important.
                    Dinah Haversham

Juanita thrust the note into the deep pocket of her blue cotton skirt. As she again turned toward the door, Steven said, "My radio!"

"Oh yes, Juanita. Steven left his radio in

56

the car. Will you ask Kurt about it?" Her face stiffened, and no wonder. Ever since Kurt had arrived in San Ysidro with his employer, she'd been fighting off his heavy-handed advances. "I mean, will you ask Elena to ask Kurt?"

Smiling again, she nodded.

When she'd gone, I looked into the covered dish. Chicken and rice. There was also a salad of mixed vegetables, caramel custard in three small brown-glazed pots, milk for the boys, and a pot of coffee for me. I felt admiration for a staff which, after the confusion of only two hours before, could produce a meal like this—not to mention the far more elaborate food which, undoubtedly, would be served to Max Hind and his sister and Paul.

We'd long since finished supper, and were asking each other riddles—What did the tiger say to the catfish? What walks on five legs and speaks French?—when Juanita finally returned. She'd been waiting, she explained, for Elena to bring this message from the Contessa.

The note, written on thick creamy paper, had neither salutation nor signature. It said, in the Contessa's bold, forward-slanted hand, "I will send for you sometime tomorrow."

Well, I'd just have to wait. "And the radio?"

"Elena has gone to ask Kurt."

With my help, she placed empty dishes and folded table linen on the big tray. She was about to leave when someone knocked. I opened the door to find Kurt standing there, an octagonal wastebasket of heavy oak in his hand. He no longer wore the visored cap on his big round head, which was covered with a stubble of red-blond hair. His eyes, of that hot-looking shade of blue which often accompanies such hair, darted past me to Juanita. Then he gave me a bow—a slight, governess-sized bow.

His English, although heavily accented, was carefully grammatical. "I have been told that you inquired about the radio." He tipped the wastebasket to display its contents. Steven's transistor was now a mass of broken plastic and exposed wires. Behind me, Steven groaned, and Tommy said, "Aw-w-w!"

"I am sorry. Someone dropped it in the courtyard." Again his gaze shot past me.

I said, rather coldly, "Thank you for telling us. Good night."

He again bowed slightly, and turned away. Closing the door, I turned to meet the boys' lamentations. Down at the villa, they'd always been allowed an hour of TV or radio after supper. "Never mind. Surely I can get another one for you tomorrow." Then: "Juanita, if you'd like to stay here for a while—"

He'll be waiting for you, my eyes added.

"No thank you, Miss." I can manage him, her eyes answered. "I am one of those who are to wash dishes."

I had an appalled vision of hundreds and hundreds of dishes pouring into that ancient kitchen across the courtyard. "Well, good night, then."

When she'd gone, I said to my still-lamenting charges, "Would you like to play Old Maid?"

"No," Steven said, which relieved me, because I wasn't sure I'd put the deck of cards in my suitcase.

"Then would you like to learn more about the castle?"

"You mean explore?"

"No, not tonight. But I could go down to the library and get something to read to you. There must be books about the castle there. Would you like that?"

Steven nodded, and Tommy, who loved being read to, said, "Yes!"

I stepped out of the room, and then halted in surprise. Even though daylight still filtered through the narrow windows on the opposite side of the corridor, artificial lighting had been turned on. It consisted of neon tubing, recessed behind a strip of thick glass that ran along the entire wall of the corridor at about shoulder height. It gave off a blue-white glare reminiscent of bus station waiting rooms. Did that same glare illuminate the kitchen and laundry and other workrooms? More than likely. Again I was impressed by Max Hind's innovations, not just because they'd cost hundreds of thousands of dollars, but because obviously no considerations of appropriateness had restrained him as he wedded blatantly visible air conditioners to eleventh-century walls, and neon lighting to corridors that had once rung to the iron-sheathed feet of armored knights.

And yet, apparently, no telephones. I'd ask the Contessa about that.

I went down the worn steps. Here too a strip of neon slanted down the wall. I had to admit I was grateful for it. Since no windows illuminated the stairwell, I otherwise would have had to make the steep descent in the murkiest of light.

When I emerged from the stairwell into the lower corridor, I noticed for the first time that there was a heavy oak door set in the lefthand wall. It must lead to the library. No need to go around through the drawing room, and perhaps encounter an annoyed Contessa.

The big bronze knob turned easily in my hand. No neon lighting here, I observed thankfully as I stepped inside. I'd have hated to find that bluish glare in this handsome room, with its smell of old book bindings, and its atmosphere of ages of scholarly toil. Warm light from parchment-shaded bronze lamps bathed the thousands of book spines, and the polished mahogany table, and the man who stood before the huge fireplace, looking at the chart above it. He turned, and I saw that he was Paul Duvall.

At the villa, after our clash on the balcony that afternoon, we'd treated each other with cool correctness whenever we met. Now I said, "Good evening."

"Good evening." He didn't smile.

"Don't let me interrupt you. I just came to get some books."

"You're not interrupting. I was just about to leave."

But as he moved with his lithe athlete's stride toward the wide doorway into the drawing room, I had the distinct impression that I had interrupted him, and that he was more annoyed about it than would seem warranted.

6

MOVING TO THE fireplace, I too studied the chart. It was of parchment, now yellow with age, and displayed the plans of all three floors of Castle Estillio, plus the underground vaults and round towers. Apparently at the time of its drawing the castle had been a monastery. Except for the huge room next to this one, labeled "chapel" on the chart, and the "offices" across the courtyard, the rooms were shown as tiny cells.

I turned to the card file and pulled out the third drawer from the top. Yes, here was the classification, "Estillio, Castle of." The cards looked quite new. That meant that in all probability one of Max Hind's employees had catalogued the library. With the file's aid I soon found, on one of the lower shelves

to the right of the fireplace, the books catalogued as dealing with the castle. Most of
them, I saw, would have been placed in a
more general classification in a public library, since they weren't concerned entirely
or even primarily with Castle Estillio. Evidently the librarian had been told to place
in this classification any book which contained more than a minor mention of the
castle.

Then, to my delight, I found a paper
guidebook wedged in between two ancient
calf-bound volumes. It was the sort of pamphlet on sale to visitors at places of historical
interest throughout Europe. Its cover bore
a color photograph of Castle Estillio, and its
price, seventy-five cents, was also given in
pesetas, shillings, and francs. The date of
printing was 1964. Quite recently, then, this
ancient pile had been a tourist attraction. So
much the better for the boys. Such guidebooks are both concise and simple.

Glancing through other books, I found
them unsuited to my present purpose. Some
were in German, of which I had no knowledge. Others were in English so archaic that
I, let alone the boys, would find them hard
to puzzle out. I might look into them later,
though.

At last I found a second book to take up-stairs. It was called, *On the Trail of the Trou-badors*, it had been published by an American firm in 1887, and its style was so self-consciously robust that it made me smile. The boys would like it, though. The frontispiece bore a photograph of the author, one Josiah Ward. In rough clothing, cloth cap, and beard, with a knapsack over his shoulder, he looked every inch the gentle-manly tramp.

Carrying the pamphlet and the book, I left the library and climbed through the bluish neon glow to the second floor. I'd almost reached the boys' room when I came to a sudden stop, arrested by the sight of some-thing which, in the confusion of our arrival this afternoon, I hadn't noticed.

At its eastern end, this corridor had been walled up with what looked like white ce-ment.

Moving quietly lest the boys hear my foot-steps pass their door, I walked to the end of the corridor. Yes, the wall was cement, and must have been erected quite recently, since its surface was fresh and white.

I stared at it for a moment. Then I swiftly retraced my steps, turned left onto the west-ern side of the quadrangle, and then left again. Yes, there at the end of the passage was another expanse of cement.

No need to go up to the unoccupied third floor. I was sure that there too I'd find the eastern side of the castle walled off. And downstairs, although Juanita hadn't said so, there must be a guard posted to keep any unauthorized person from wandering into forbidden territory.

Why? Guardhouses and a gate to turn back uninvited visitors might possibly be understandable. But why should Max Hind take these measures to exclude from a part of the structure all but those few servants necessary to his and his sister's comfort?

As I stared at the cement wall, bathed in that bluish glow, I felt my palms turn cold. It was like that moment when a dream, only vaguely troubling until then, subtly alters. The dream landscape darkens and changes shape, the air thickens, and you know, helplessly, that soon something bad, very bad, is going to happen.

Then I gave myself a mental shake. If anything "bad" was going to happen, would those two coldly sane egotists, Julia Ascoli and Paul Duvall, have set foot within ten miles of here? Because it was expedient, they'd go along with Max Hind up to a point, but only up to a point. The moment his aberrations threatened them with danger, or even serious discomfort, they'd call a halt.

I retraced my steps slowly, giving my quickened heart beats time to subside, and my face time to rearrange itself into a calm smile.

I found both boys leaning out the casement window. Turning, Steven said, "You were gone a long time!"

Glancing out the window, I saw that an arc light, apparently somewhere up on the battlements, had been turned on, bathing the cobblestones in a bright glow. The inner pair of iron-sheathed gates had been closed. Undoubtedly those at the other end of the tunnel had been closed too. I said, "I had trouble finding the right books."

Settling in a chair, with the boys cross-legged on the floor, I opened the tourist pamphlet.

"Castle Estillio," it said, "was built during the latter half of the eleventh century by the Counts of Estillio, on the northeastern end of a tableland which rises abruptly from the plain. Its granite stones were dug from a quarry, long since filled in, near the castle's site. On its northern and eastern sides, the castle was built so close to the mesa's edge that a ledge less than two feet wide separates the castle's base from the cliff plunging steeply to the plain below.

("I want to go look!" Steven said, and I said, "In the morning. You couldn't see anything in the dark, anyway.")

"In the twelfth century the Estillio family died out, and the castle passed into other hands. For many years in the fifteenth century the castle stood abandoned. One can imagine that local peasants stabled their domestic animals in the courtyard, and appropriated whatever furniture they could find for firewood.

"In the sixteenth century the castle became a monastery for the Carthusian Order. The peaceful monks tore down the semicircular wall which protected the castle on its western and southern flanks, filled in the fosse ("That was a big ditch," I told the boys), and substituted heavy oak doors, sheathed with iron, for the portcullis. ("That was a kind of heavy grating which could slide down to bar the entrance.")

"After a little more than a century, the monks too abandoned the castle, and it became Crown property. During the Napoleonic Invasion, it was used as an arsenal. Later the government sold it to a private individual. Changing hands several times during the nineteenth century and the first half of the twentieth, it is now the property of Señor Guillermo Guerrero of Madrid.

"Entering the castle by a tunnel which runs through the entire southern side of the quadrangle, the visitor finds himself in a cobblestoned courtyard—"

The pamphlet went on to describe the rest of the castle, including the round towers with their winding stairs and arrow slits. Evidently then, as now, the castle's eastern side had housed the owner's private quarters, because the guidebook stated that part, though not all, of that section was closed to the public.

"The visitor will find postcards, souvenirs, and a snack bar serving tea and sandwiches at moderate prices in a room adjoining the dining hall." That, I realized, must have been the room now labeled "billiard room" on the chart in the downstairs corridor. "Castle Estillio is open to the public on Tuesdays and Thursdays, from 9 A.M. to 5 P.M., from May through October."

Poor Mr. Guerrero, I thought. What financial disaster had forced him to open those iron-sheathed gates to hordes of camera-toting tourists? And apparently he'd still had to sell his castle eventually—probably to the Greek shipowner from whom, according to Julia Ascoli, her brother had bought it.

Tommy asked, "Will they come next Tuesday?"

"Who, dear?"

"The visitors. And can we get some tea and sandwiches at the snack bar?"

Steven snorted. I gave him a stern look. I was going to have to do something about those snorts. "No, Tommy. There's no snack bar now. Your uncle doesn't admit the public."

Laying the pamphlet aside, I picked up Mr. Josiah Ward's book, and found the chapter on Castle Estillio. At the time of his visit, 1886, the castle's absentee owner, an Englishman, had left it in charge of a single caretaker.

"The old fellow who finally opened the gate to my knocking," Mr. Ward wrote, "seemed reluctant to let me in. Perhaps the garb I'd donned for the Open Road struck him as ruffianly. But after a while the man-to-man manner in which I addressed him, or perhaps the coin I pressed into his gnarled hand, caused him to swing the gates wide open.

"In the cobblestoned courtyard, I gazed

for a while at the ancient battlements, lost in thoughts of days when Knights Were Bold. Then the old fellow plucked my sleeve, and we set out on our tour."

His guide had taken him to one of the round towers first. Then they'd worked their way down through "ancient storerooms and splendidly furnished modern apartments, although not much more splendid, and certainly far less comfortable, than I have seen on Beacon Hill in my native Boston."

They'd ended up in the kitchen. "My guide told me that the local peasantry had a legend that the huge fireplace concealed a secret entrance to an ancient tunnel. In olden times, the castle's defenders could creep through the tunnel, emerge at the foot of the mesa, and take their attackers by surprise. He'd never been able to find the secret entrance, nor could I, although I ran my hands over the dusty bricks for at least fifteen minutes. Perhaps it is just as well. If a section of the masonry had swung back, probably I would have lacked courage to descend to the subterranean depths thus revealed.

"The afternoon was waning. I said good-bye to my new friend, hoisted my knapsack to my shoulder, and, whistling a merry tune, set out on my next adventure."

I closed the book. Tommy asked, "Do you think there is a tunnel?"

"I doubt it." Seeing his face fall, I added, "It's possible, though. I suppose it would have been a good way to take attackers by surprise."

"Do you think he'd have been scared to go down there?"

"The man who wrote this book? I doubt it."

"He wouldn't have said it," Steven suddenly offered, "if he'd thought people would believe he was scared. He just wanted to sound—"

"Modest?" I suggested, and he nodded.

I looked at him thoughtfully. Sometimes the elder of my boys displayed a shrewdness, a grasp of adult motives, that almost frightened me.

"Well, bedtime, boys." They made a few feeble protests, which I ignored. Grumbling was as much a part of the bedtime ritual as baths and teeth brushing.

To escape my still uneasy thoughts, I read three more chapters of Mr. Ward's book after I'd put the boys to bed. When I felt drowsy enough to sleep, I turned off my bedside lamp.

The silence was complete. No sound of

voices, no footfalls, penetrated the thick walls. The floodlight in the courtyard had been turned out. On this moonless night, my casement window opened onto utter blackness. This might have been one of those nights hundreds of years before, when this ancient structure stood abandoned.

I thought of those years. Ravens nesting in the round towers. Wild, four-footed creatures padding across the courtyard cobblestones. Wind keening through narrow windows to stir the rotted remnants of a wall tapestry—

My thoughts blurred, and I slept.

A sound directly overhead awoke me. A muted clangor, as of some heavy metal object rolling across a stone floor. No, I thought, still confused with sleep, it wasn't the rolling sound that had awakened me. A moment earlier there'd been a louder noise, although still muted.

In the room above, some object had fallen, an object heavy enough that I'd heard the crash through the stone ceiling. What had caused it to fall? A rat? A prowling cat? No, a small animal could never dislodge anything that heavy.

Someone had been searching those storerooms on the third floor. And recalling Paul

Duvall's eagerness to come to this place, and his annoyance when I interrupted his scrutiny of that ancient parchment in the library, I was sure who the searcher was.

7

EVEN THOUGH I'D had trouble getting back to sleep, I awoke early the next morning, as I almost always do in a strange place. Slipping into my robe, I went to the casement window. The iron-sheathed gates were still closed. Except for its western extremity, the courtyard lay in blue shadow. From the windows of what must be the kitchen came the sound of voices, and a muffled clatter of crockery.

The kitchen door opened, and a woman shooed a big orange cat onto the cobblestones. Bristling with outrage, he stalked a few paces, then sat down, stretched his left rear leg, and began to groom his stomach. The woman lingered in the doorway, watching the cat. I too watched him, remembering that sound in the night which might have been caused, but probably wasn't, by some prowling animal.

The woman went back in. I looked at my

wrist watch. Six-twenty. If I hurried, I could look at the floor above before it was time to wake the boys.

About fifteen minutes later I climbed the narrow stairs. When I reached the landing, I saw ahead of me a door that undoubtedly led to the northwestern round tower. It stood partly open. I could see the foot of a spiral stairwell, so narrow that I gave a shudder. The human race was smaller when those stairs were built. Now a broad-shouldered man could have negotiated them only by turning sideways.

I looked at the corridor's eastern end. Yes, here too was a cement wall, barring access to the whole eastern side of the quadrangle. Moving quickly and quietly, I passed the first three doors, and opened the fourth.

Here the leaded casement windows were closed. Daylight filtered only dimly through the cobwebs and grime of many years. But I could see the rolled-up carpets, standing on end like clustered smokestacks, and a chest of age-darkened oak, about six feet long and three feet wide. I could see, too, what had made the clatter in the night.

Apparently the suit of armor had stood behind the chest, because the metal feet and legs still lay there. The rest was scattered over the stone floor. The casque, or helmet, had rolled at least ten feet, coming to rest near the group of rugs.

Stooping, I picked up a greave, the piece designed to protect the foreleg. Instantly, I saw it wasn't genuine, but a light, recently manufactured reproduction, probably made of some aluminum alloy. Movie companies, I reflected, probably ordered such reproductions in carload lots for those vast spectacles they'd been filming in Europe for as long as I could remember.

The casque was the only part of scattered armor which could have been genuine. When I picked it up I found it heavy, at least five pounds, and beautifully incised above the visor in a gilly-flower pattern. But whether it really was ancient, or just a careful reproduction, I had no way of telling.

How had it come to be here? I could think of one explanation. Perhaps the hard-up Señor Guerrero of Madrid had bought this spurious suit of armor to lend atmosphere on those Tuesdays and Thursdays when the castle was open to the public. Later the Greek shipping tycoon, or Max Hind or one of his employees, had disdainfully banished it to this storeroom.

But what had toppled it from its position behind that chest?

Turning to the chest I saw almost instantly that it had been forcibly opened. A jimmy, inserted on either side of the lock, had left fresh scars on the dark wood. Using both hands, I lifted the heavy lid and let it fall back until it lay parallel with the stone floor. Yes, undoubtedly it was that lid which had set the fake armor crashing.

The chest held heavy velvet draperies, perhaps once neatly folded, but now in wild disarray. I plunged both arms deep in the chest and felt around. My hands encountered no solid object. When rising dust made me sneeze, I hastily stood up and closed the lid.

Had the chest held what Paul Duvall searched for? And if it hadn't, had he gone on, taking greater care to be silent, to the other storerooms along this corridor? I'd like to have seen if those rooms also showed signs of recent disturbance. But that would have to wait. It was almost time to wake the boys.

I lingered for a moment, though, staring at the chest. Was it my duty to tell the Contessa about this? Undoubtedly. But in this case I had no intention of doing my duty.

Casting aspersions on Paul Duvall probably would bring me instant dismissal, and a one-way ride to the airport of my choice. Even months ago, parting from the boys would have been a painful wrench. To leave them now in this isolated place, helpless in the hands of their oddly behaved uncle and indifferent aunt, was quite unthinkable.

Closing the door silently, I stepped out into the corridor. I noticed then that no neon tubing, protected by heavy glass, ran along the wall up here. In fact, there were no light fixtures at all. He must have made his search by flashlight.

Crossing to the outer wall, I stepped into a window embrasure, pushed the narrow casement panes apart, and looked down. Yes, just as the guidebook had said, only a narrow ledge of earth separated the castle's base from the vertical plunge of the mesa's northern wall. With a thrill of vicarious terror, I pictured a workman of almost a thousand years ago, standing on that narrow ledge to press mortar between rough squares of granite. Surely those long-dead men must have been secured by ropes as they piled stone upon stone. But surely, also, there had been accidents, just as there almost always were during the construction of modern skyscrapers. In my mind's eye I saw a human figure grow smaller and smaller as it plummeted backward toward the plain, horror-filled face upturned to the sky. In my mind's ear I heard a scream from a throat long since turned to dust—

Dizzy, I backed out of the embrasure and turned toward the stairs leading down.

8

EMERGING INTO THE lower floor corridor, I saw Juanita standing at my bedroom door, fist poised to knock. She turned, smiled, and called a greeting. Then, as her gaze traveled from my face to my hands and back again, I saw puzzlement in her brown eyes. I looked at my grimy palms. Evidently my face was dirt-streaked, too.

I said in a low voice, "I've done a little exploring." No need to ask her not to tell anyone. Juanita and I understood each other.

She said, "I thought was possible you oversleeped. Soon I will bring the breakfasts."

"Thank you, Juanita."

Going into my room, I hastily washed my hands and face and then went in to wake the boys. Half an hour later we were at breakfast—orange juice for three, porridge for the boys, and scrambled eggs and toast and coffee for me.

When Juanita came to take the plates, I asked, "Did you hear anything in the night? Any sound from the third floor?"

"No, miss." Her eyes added, so that's why you went up there.

"Steven, Tommy, did either of you leave your room last night?"

Steven looked indignant, and rightfully so. "We'd never do that. We promised we wouldn't."

"I apologize. But I thought I heard something—"

"Ghosts," Steven said with relish.

Tommy looked frightened. I said, "There's no such thing as a ghost. It must have been a cat prowling around, or a rat."

The boys seemed to accept that, and so did Juanita, who'd drawn in her breath sharply at the word rat.

When Juanita had left, Steven said, "Can we explore now?"

"Lessons first." Ignoring their groans—I think they'd hoped that their schoolbooks, like their toys, had been packed in some as yet undelivered trunk—I went into the next room and came back with two arithmetic texts and one on American history.

For two and a half hours I kept them at their books. Then I said, "All right. Put your books and papers on that shelf over there."

They were scrambling to obey when someone knocked. Two burly menservants in dark blue cotton work clothes stood out in the corridor beside a big leather trunk. In it Juanita and I, two days before, had packed a number of Steven and Tommy's toys, including most of their electric train system. The men carried the trunk inside, placed it at my direction against one wall, and left. Wild to get out of the room, the boys didn't want to even glance inside the trunk. "Let's at least take the softball and bat out onto the mesa with us."

They agreed enthusiastically. Down at the villa I'd described baseball to them—after all, they were half-American—and had introduced the game of batter-up. We hadn't been able to enjoy it much, though. The villa's walled rear garden had been small for the game, and filled with shatterable statuary. But out on the hard-packed soil of the mesa, we could hit fungoes to our hearts' content.

With Steven carrying the bat and Tommy

the ball, we left the room. Immediately Steven darted across the corridor to an embrasure, pushed the casement panes farther apart, and poked his head out. "It's down there! I see the ledge!"

Steven stepped back, and I boosted Tommy up to look. When I'd set his little brother down, Steven asked, "Why didn't they build the castle right on the edge of the cliff?"

"I'm not sure. Maybe they were looking ahead. Maybe they thought that after hundreds of years, erosion would have worn the cliff's face away until the castle's base would overhang it. Erosion," I added, "is the wearing away of soil by wind and water."

We moved along the corridor. When we reached the stairwell Steven said, "Let's go up to the next floor. Maybe we can see some rats."

"I should hope not. Anyway, I'll have to ask your aunt's permission before I take you up there. Now let's get out onto the mesa, where we can get a good view of the castle."

With no more protest, the boys clattered ahead of me down the stairs and along the corridor, where I glanced into that luxurious drawing room. It seemed to be empty except for two maids wielding dustcloths. In the courtyard we saw that the big inner gates had been opened. With the boys still in the lead we went through the tunnel and between the opened outer gates. Then, as I had the afternoon before, both boys stopped short, staring at those red sentry boxes down the road, and the barred gate that linked them.

Steven asked, "What's that?"

I said lightly, "Something your uncle put up to keep strangers out. After all, this whole mesa belongs to the castle. We read that in the guidebook last night."

"But he's got those big heavy doors at each end of the tunnel—"

"Perhaps he wants uninvited visitors turned back before they even reach the castle. Come on. Let's play ball."

We struck off at right angles to the road, toward the mesa's western edge, pausing now and then to watch a hawk circle against the blue, or to admire the yellow-flowered cacti which, along with gray-green chaparral and occasional groups of juniper, sprang from the hard ocher soil. About two hundred yards from the castle we stopped. Tommy found a couple of stout sticks. With them we drew home plate, the pitcher's box, and the base.

Steven took first turn at bat, with me guarding the base. His little brother, lower lip thrust out in concentration, threw the softball straight over the plate. Steven's bat caught it solidly. The ball soared high over the pitcher's box, dropped to earth, and rolled over the hard ground into a clump of juniper. Short legs pumping, Tommy raced after it, while I waited for the toss I knew wouldn't come in time.

Steven had touched base and returned triumphantly to the plate when we heard Tommy's yell. Anxiously I ran ahead of Steven to the clump of juniper. We found Tommy sitting under a tree, right hand gripping his right shin. "That darned old thing tripped me!"

I looked at the weathered metal pipe, about half a foot in diameter, which projected some fourteen inches above the ground. It had a peaked cap, held in place by metal strips about four inches long, thus allowing air space between the cap and the top of the pipe. I said, "Let me see your leg."

He took his hand away. "You'll have a bruise, but the skin isn't broken."

"What is it?" Steven was staring at the pipe.

"I haven't the faintest notion."

"Maybe someone was going to put a well here."

I looked at him, impressed. For all I knew, people did sometimes test for a water table by sinking a pipe into the earth.

Tommy said, again nursing his shin, "Maybe they needed a well because they were going to build another castle here."

Steven snorted. "That's not how you start to build a castle."

"Steven, stop that snorting! It's very unattractive. And what do any of us know about how one starts to build a castle?"

Muttering that he was sorry, he stooped, picked up a pebble, and dropped it down the pipe. After a moment I heard it, or thought I heard it, strike against rock.

Tommy had stood up. "Do you want to go in?" I asked.

His tone was manful. "No, I can play."

With Tommy limping ostentatiously for a few steps, and then forgetting about it, we started back toward our improvised playing field. We were almost there when I heard angry voices from over on the road.

Shading my eyes with my hand, I gazed at the red sports car which had stopped before the red sentry boxes, and at the yellow-haired man who stood beside it. He was talking to the two guards, or rather, to judge by the irate voices and wild gesticulations of all three men, arguing with them. As I watched, one of the guards shoved the blond man's shoulder, and he shoved back.

My heart gave a glad, incredulous leap. I was sure that the red car was a four-year-old Triumph. What was more important, I was sure I knew its driver.

9

WHEN THE BOYS and I were about a hundred feet away, one of the guards saw us. Stopping their argument, all three men turned and watched our approach. The blond man smiled at me and said, "Hi."

He was thin, wiry, and about five feet ten in height. His eyes were gray. There was a faint scar across the bridge of his nose. It was, I knew, the result of a fall from a tree house in Ladesville, Wisconsin, when he was eight.

"Hello, Len. What are you—?" Then: "Your arm!"

He'd rolled the left sleeve of his plaid sport shirt high on his arm. Just above his elbow was a tourniquet made of a twisted hand-kerchief. Below it, his heavily tanned fore-arm was streaked with blood.

He said, with a rueful expression, "I got it by being a Good Samaritan. Next time I'll pass on the other side. Look, Dinah. Can you persuade these jokers to let me through? I need medical attention."

"You certainly do," I said somewhat queasily. I don't faint at the sight of blood, but I don't like it much. Turning to the guards, I said in Spanish, "You must let this man pass. He's hurt."

The guards looked back at me unhappily but stubbornly. The elder, a thickset man of about forty, with what ordinarily must have been a pleasant face, said doggedly, "We have our orders. No one must pass."

Apparently Len understood that, because he whipped a wallet from his hip pocket, laid it on the Triumph's hood, and began to extract cards from it. He handed the first one to me. It was his accreditation from Universal Press. "Give them this," he said. "And this." It was his press card from a Philadelphia daily. "And this." It had been issued by a weekly published in Manchester, England.

"I've tried arguing with them," he said.

"Now will you try? Tell them I've got more, but that ought to do it. Tell them to tell their boss that if I don't get in, about fifty million people are going to know that Max Hind turned a man away to bleed to death on the road."

My lips quirked. There was little danger of his bleeding to death. Except for a thin oozing, the blood on his arm had already dried. I turned to the elder of the guards, and handed him Len's identification. The portentous expression with which he gazed at the top card made me think he couldn't even read Spanish, let alone English.

"Mr. Carstairs is a newspaperman," I explained. "Those are his press cards. Have someone take them to Mr. Hind, and tell him that Mr. Carstairs has a wound that needs dressing." No need to repeat Len's threat about fifty million readers. Max Hind would understand the import of those cards.

The cards in his hand, the guard turned and walked up the road. The younger guard, returning to his sentry box, stared at us with mingled belligerence and unease.

I said to Len, "What on earth are you doing here?"

"I'm on vacation."

"Yes, I know. But why are you here?"

He smiled, gray eyes looking directly into mine. "I told you we'd see each other again soon."

To my dismay I felt my face growing warm. I, who since the age of fifteen had prided myself on my cool, was blushing.

With a start of belated recollection, I turned to the boys. Side by side, ramrod straight, they stared at Len with the same bleak hostility I'd seen in their faces that day I met them. "Oh, no!" I thought, appalled.

"Len, this is Steven Marsden, and this is his brother Tommy. Boys, this is Mr. Carstairs."

As they'd been taught, the boys in turn stepped forward, shook hands, and said, "How do you do, sir?" Steven paused between "do" and "sir" just long enough to make the title sound insulting.

Looking at me, Len lifted a quizzical eyebrow. I shook my head slightly.

Turning to the car, he drew a lap robe from the well behind the bucket seats. "Let's all sit down, huh? I'm a wounded man, remember."

He spread the robe in the narrow shade cast by the car, and we sat down. The boys—cross-legged, wooden-faced, hostile-eyed—might have been captive children raised from an early age by one of the more warlike Indian tribes.

I said, "What happened to your arm?"

"Oh, I picked up a hitch-hiker less than an hour ago. We'd gone about a mile when he pulled a knife on me and demanded my wallet. I think," he said, with a quick side glance at my charges, "that he was a gypsy."

I also looked at the boys. They were struggling, not too successfully, to keep their faces expressionless. I said nothing. Len said nothing. The silence lengthened.

Steven asked in a bored voice, "What happened then?"

"Oh, I slugged him, took his knife away, and threw him out of the car. But he'd cut me. When he first turned on me with the knife, I automatically threw up my arm to protect my face, and he slashed it."

"Oh." Steven still managed to sound bored, but his little brother stared at Len with open awe. I sensed that neither of them, though, was any more reconciled to Len's presence. In fact, learning the formidable nature of the interloper had only increased their hostility.

They hadn't been with me that morning nearly a week ago when I'd met Len. Since it was my day off, I'd left them at the villa in Juanita's care. Pleasantly aware of sunlight, of hibiscus flowers scarlet against white villa walls, and of the beach and sparkling sea at the foot of the sloping street, I'd walked for about a hundred yards, turned right along another street, and entered the town square.

Two of the Beautiful People were there. A slender brunette woman in white pants and a Pucci blouse sat at a sidewalk cafe. In one of the Contessa's magazines, I'd seen a photograph of the woman and her debutante daughter and Princess Grace, posing in the palace gardens at Monaco. The woman's much-lifted face had the blank perfection of a doll's. Beside her sat a man so deeply tanned that it was impossible to tell whether he was old or young, in magnificent health or sickly.

But not even the presence of those two could mar the unpretentious charm of this square, with its town pump that some San Ysidrians still used, its small white stucco church, its half dozen shops with their brightly striped awnings, and its newsstand.

I headed straight for the stand. If possible, I wanted to buy a guidebook to the region in which Castle Estillio was situated. An aged woman sat behind the counter, knitting a gray scarf.

As I browsed through the guidebooks in the rack, I became aware that a red Triumph had stopped before the pharmacy, and that a young man had got out. Somehow I felt sure that he was an American, although I couldn't have said why. His informal garb, chino pants and a blue pullover, might have been worn by a young man of any nationality.

He went into the pharmacy. A few minutes later, while he was still in the shop, I settled upon my purchase. Placing my handbag upon the counter, I opened it and took out my coin purse. At that moment a heavy truck, crossing the square, backfired only a few feet behind me. I jumped, and my elbow struck the opened handbag, knocking it from the counter. Lipstick, compact, ballpoint pen, and a few stray coins scattered in all directions over the cobblestones. Stooping, I picked up my handbag and refilled it with my possessions. I'd turned back to the counter when a voice said in horribly accented Spanish, "Is not this yours also?"

The young man was holding out the guidebook. Evidently I'd managed to dislodge it from the counter too. "Thank you," I said, in English. "It will be mine, when I pay for it."

He smiled widely. "So you're American. Same here."

When I'd paid for the book, he was still standing there. "Will you have something to drink with me?" He nodded toward the cafe, not the one where the Beautiful People sat, but the one next to it. There all the round tables under the striped awning were empty.

What a nice face, under the sun-streaked blond hair. The forehead with its two horizontal creases. The smile that lit up his gray eyes. Still—"Thank you," I said, "but I'm afraid not."

He stood there, apparently nonplussed, for a moment, and then reached into his hip pocket. "You mean, you don't know anything about me." He opened a leather carrying case. "Passport," he said, extending it to me. Automatically I took it, and then just stood there, feeling foolish. "Philadelphia Banner press card, Universal News press card—"

That did it. I said, looking down at his photograph and the name, Len Carstairs, "My parents were Joe and Diana Haversham."

After a long moment he said, "They were

good. They were very good. I met them once. Five years ago, at a press conference in Paris. I'd been a correspondent for only a few months then. They were damned nice to me."

My throat tightened. "Yes, they were nice people."

"Will you have that drink with me?"

"Yes, thank you."

We crossed to the cafe, where we agreed it was too early for anything stronger than tea. When the waiter had taken our order back to the kitchen, Len lit a cigarette and asked, "What's your name besides Haversham, what are you doing in this town, and why"—he turned the guidebook so that he could read its title—"did you buy this?"

"Dinah. I'm a governess here. And I'm going up to that part of the country in a few days."

"Governess!"

"Don't say it in that tone. I meet other governesses on the beach. Not many of them are the scrawny spinsters you read about."

"I can see you're not scrawny. But you are a spinster, aren't you?"

"I am." It had been only mock anxiety in his voice, but it had pleased me.

"Whom do you govern?"

"The Contessa Ascoli's nephews."

He dropped his cigarette onto the table. "Damn," he said, snuffing it out in the ashtray. "Isn't she the sister of that Texas multimillionaire?" He snapped his fingers. "Hines? Haines?"

"Hind, Max Hind. Yes, she is."

"But you're leaving her now?"

"Leaving? Oh, the guidebook. Oh, no. I'm going with the Contessa and her brother and the two boys up to Castle Estillio. Her brother owns it."

"Sure. I read about that. Sounded as if he were turning it into the Hind Hilton." He paused. "How did you get to be a governess? Is there some kind of course you can take?"

"For all I know, there is. But it didn't happen that way with me."

Before I knew it, I was telling him about that bleak December day in Paris. I even mentioned the dead leaf, plastered against the Brasserie Lipp's glass enclosure.

"But you won't go on being a governess, will you?"

"Of course not. I'll go back and get my Master's or—do something else with my life." After all, I couldn't spend it raising Steven and Tommy, and yet the very thought of leaving them—

To blot out that thought, I said, "Your turn. How did you get to be a European correspondent?"

He told me. High school correspondent for his local paper in Ladesville, Wisconsin. Editor of his college paper at a Pennsylvania university. A job on a Philadelphia daily after graduation. A vacation trip to Paris during a wave of strikes, and a brash cable back to his paper, saying that he was "on the spot," and would like to send them the story. Their favorable reply.

"From then on it was easy. Universal also accredited me, and then a couple of English papers."

Thinking of my own childhood, much of it spent wandering with my parents all over Europe, I asked, "What was it like, growing up in a small town?"

"Great." He told me about the Little League, and skating on Mirror Lake, and that fall from the tree house which had scarred his nose.

At last, glancing at my watch, I said, "I've got to get back!" Ordinarily I spent my day off well away from the villa, on the theory that I needed a complete break in my routine. But today I had to start packing for our trek to Castle Estillio.

"I'll drive you," he said.

As the little car carried us up the sloping street, I asked, "Are you covering a story here?"

"In San Ysidro? Lord, no. I'm on vacation. Free as a breeze for a month—well, a month minus three days."

When we stopped before the villa I said, "Goodbye, Len. And thanks."

"Not goodbye. See you. We'll be seeing each other soon."

At the time, I'd thought he meant that he'd get in touch with me after I returned to San Ysidro. And yet, unbelievably, he was here now, sitting with me and the boys in the Triumph's scant shade.

Unbelievably. Could I, after little more than an hour in that cafe, have lingered so strongly in his thoughts that he'd follow me up here? The idea was pleasant, more pleasant than I liked to admit, and yet—

"Here comes Cerberus," he said.

The elder of the guards was coming down the road, more rapidly than he'd gone up it. As he drew closer, I saw that his broad peasant face wore a relieved smile.

Extending the press cards to Len, he said, "The señor is permitted to enter."

10

THE FOUR OF us rode up to the castle in the Triumph. When Len said, "Hop in, fellas," Steven at first remained motionless. Then, perhaps unwilling to leave the field to the enemy for even a few minutes, he climbed into the well behind the bucket seats. Tommy rode on my lap, his gaze fixed unswervingly on Len's profile. I put my arm around him. He didn't resist, but neither did he relax against my shoulder with a contented sigh, as he did sometimes when he forgot he was a big boy of six.

Their alarmed hostility was only natural, I reflected. In a very important sense they had no one but me in the whole world. I'd just have to reassure them that I wasn't about to disappear over the horizon with this gypsy-fighter-sprung-from-nowhere.

We entered the courtyard. A woman almost six feet tall, wearing a nurse's uniform, stood a few yards beyond the inner gate, large feet in their white shoes planted firmly on the cobblestones. "That's Mr. Hind's private nurse," I murmured.

"Man! Could she hunt tigers with a switch!"

As we were getting out of the car, the woman approached and said, "You must be Mr. Carstairs." Her gaze went professionally to his bloodied arm. "I'm Miss Walmsey, Mr. Hind's nurse. Leave your car here, please, and come to the surgery."

Turning, she walked briskly toward the southeast corner of the courtyard. Len gave the boys and me a grimace of mock terror, and then followed her. They entered the door to a room which, on the corridor chart, had been labeled "su." So that was what "su" had meant.

The boys and I started to our own quarters. As we moved along the corridor toward the stairs, Steven asked, "Who is he?"

"A newspaperman. I don't know him very well. We met in San Ysidro last week."

"When? That morning you went out alone?"

"Yes."

Perhaps reflecting upon the folly of letting one's governess out of one's sight, both boys remained silent the rest of the way to their room. "Wash your hands," I said. "Juanita will be bringing lunch in about half an hour."

But it was only a few minutes later that she tapped on the door. Instantly I saw that she'd been crying. Her dark eyes were reddened and her pretty face slightly swollen. The Contessa's personal maid, she told me, had said that the Contessa wanted to see me in her rooms.

"Right now?"

"Yes, Miss."

"Juanita, what's troubling you?"

She lapsed into Spanish. "Oh, señorita! I shall not see my mother and sister. I have no day off. No one has, while we are here. Instead we will all receive triple pay one day a week. Many of the others are pleased. But I—" She broke off, eyes filling with tears.

I felt a surge of anger. Here was one more thing I'd ask Julia Ascoli about.

"I'm sorry," I said, "but maybe you should be glad. Just think, triple pay! With that you can buy fine presents for your mother and sister. When we get back to the villa, I'll try to persuade the Contessa to give you several days off, so you can visit your village."

She brightened a little. "Thank you."

"I'd better go to the Contessa now."

Telling the boys I'd be back soon, I followed Juanita down the stairs and along the corridor to where other stairs—not blocked off here by a cement wall—rose to the second floor of the eastern, or family, side of the quadrangle.

I'd been right in my supposition that a guard would be posted here. In a chair tipped back against the wall, a handsome man of about thirty sat where he could keep an eye on the stairs, on the corridor down which Juanita and I had come, and on the corridor stretching south along the castle's eastern side. A few feet away along that corridor, I could see, through its iron fretwork housing, Max Hind's elevator. Its size surprised me. I'd pictured it as only large enough to accommodate two or three persons. Instead it was about the size of a freight elevator.

The guard wasn't alone. Elena, the Contessa's personal maid, stood talking to him. Their conversation had been flirtatious, to judge by the smile lingering on her lips as she turned to Juanita and me. She was a thin woman of thirty-odd, good-looking in a sharp-faced way. I'd never liked her. She had that cynical, faintly corrupt air I'd observed before in personal maids, valets, and others in intimate service to the very rich. It was as if, learning that even their powerful employers had weaknesses, they could have no esteem whatever for lesser mortals.

She said to Juanita in Spanish, "You can go back now." Then to me in English, "I'll take you to the Contessa, Miss Haversham." Her manner was indifferent almost, but not quite, to the point of rudeness.

I followed her up the stairs, which were as badly worn as those leading to the boys' quarters and mine. On the second floor, though, I stepped into a different world. Here rich carpeting, of classic Aubusson design but obviously recent manufacture, covered the corridor flagstones. The walls had been paneled with dark oiled wood. The vaulted ceiling had been left bare, but crystal chandeliers hung from it. No neon tubing here.

Elena stopped before a door, knocked. When Julia Ascoli's voice responded, the maid opened the door. "Here is Miss Haversham, Contessa," she said, and walked away.

I stepped inside. This room, also paneled with dark wood, obviously was the Contessa's sitting room. In a tapestry-covered chair, beside a small gilt table, she sat very erect, with a cold, I-mean-business look in her brown eyes.

"Good morning," she said. Then, in the same breath, "Who's that Carstairs man?"

This interview, I saw, wasn't going to turn out as I had planned. At the very start, I was the one on the defensive.

"He's a journalist."

"We know that," she said impatiently. "But who *is* he? Do you know him?"

"Not very well." I explained about the guidebook, the spilled handbag, and the conversation over tea at that sidewalk cafe.

"So he followed you up here." Her tone now was touched with amused envy. "Oh, to be your age again." Then, coldly: "Well, I suppose it couldn't be helped. But my brother was annoyed, very annoyed indeed." She paused. "Well, it must be almost time for your lunch."

It was dismissal. "Contessa, I wrote you a note, and you sent one back saying you'd see me today—"

"That's right. What with all this fuss over that Carstairs person, I'd forgotten about it." Despite her casual tone, I sensed she was on her guard now. "What did you want to see me about?"

So many things—My groping thoughts seized upon one. "Those sentries down on the road. Why are they there?"

"That's a private road. My brother doesn't want nosy tourists driving right up to the castle." She didn't add that it was none of my business, but her tone did. "Is that all, Miss Haversham?"

I stood my ground. "No. I wondered about telephones. I haven't seen any."

After a moment she said, "My brother ordered most of the phones taken out before we came up here."

I waited. After a moment she went on, with unconcealed annoyance, "After he'd hired that mob of servants, he couldn't leave phones all over the place. Too many people would be sneaking long distance calls. My brother's a rich man, but even the rich like to draw the line somewhere. And in case of emergency, there are phones in his rooms and mine that can be used."

Should I test her on that? Wait a day or two, and then give her some urgent reason why I had to call my grandparents in North Dakota, or some ex-classmate in Paris? No, better not. She'd know I was testing. So far, I'd been a great convenience to her. Whole days had passed at the villa without her even seeing her nephews. But the moment I became more annoying than useful, she'd dismiss me, and turn the boys over to Juanita.

For a few minutes longer, though, I had to risk being an irritant. "About Juanita, Contessa. Her village is near here. She's so looked forward to seeing her mother and sister. Couldn't she go?"

The Contessa picked up a cigarette from a crystal box on the small gilt table beside her, lit it with a gold lighter, and set the lighter down. "I'll be frank with you, although I don't want you to tell this to the children, or anyone else. We can't have a panic starting here. But anyway, there's a hepatitis outbreak in this part of the country. My brother didn't hear of it until after all the preparations for coming up here had been made. We can't have the servants wandering all over the countryside, and bringing infection back with them. That's why my brother is giving triple pay instead of days off. And I think it's very generous of him. After all, he's protecting them from the disease, too."

Was there a hepatitis outbreak? And if so, was Max Hind so afraid of the disease that he'd tried to seal off himself and his family and his servants from the outside world? Perhaps. The fact that he, who appeared quite hale except for his useless legs, kept an R.N.

in his permanent employ might indicate a streak of hypochondria.

Then I realized that the hepatitis outbreak, whether or not it existed, wasn't the reason for the canceled days off, and the guards down on the road. There was some other reason. I knew that, because it was obvious that she was lying to me.

Probably Julia Ascoli hadn't had much practice in lying. People usually lie because they are afraid, or to secure some advantage. Ever since the age of eleven, she'd had all the advantages, and little reason to fear anything or anyone. Consequently, as she'd just proved, she was a very bad liar. Her voice had sounded forced, and her eyes had a watchful, defensive shine.

"I see." Then, after a pause: "Steven's radio was broken. Could he have another? And the boys are used to their own TV set. Could one be placed in their room?"

"I'm afraid not. My brother loathes radio and TV, especially here. He feels it doesn't fit in with the atmosphere."

Air conditioning, neon lighting, and an elevator, but no radio or TV.

I must have let my unbelief show, because two spots of color appeared on her cheekbones. She said, "If there's nothing else—"

There was. That cement walling off the eastern side of the quadrangle on the second and third floors, for instance. But she'd only lie to me, or perhaps justifiably, tell me that where her brother put cement was none of my business.

"There's just one thing I must know, Contessa." I hesitated, wondering how best to phrase it. "Mr. Hind's actions are, of course, no concern of mine, except in the way they might affect the children. And so, is there —is there any danger to the boys in this place?"

"None." She wasn't lying now. She was telling the truth, or at least what she thought was the truth. Her voice was earnest, her gaze direct.

"I realize what your opinion of me must be," she went on. Her slight smile said that my opinion hadn't cost her any sleep. "And I'm not fond of my nephews. I've never pretended to be. But neither my brother nor I would ever deliberately expose them to danger."

"Thank you. That was the one thing I really needed to know."

"And you won't mention the hepatitis outbreak? Someone like Juanita might decide her family could be ill, and try to rush to them. Even if they are ill, it's better for her that she stay away from them."

If the hepatitis outbreak was, as I felt almost certain, a fabrication, a sort of cover story, then surely it was Max Hind who'd made it up. His sister was too lazy-minded to have done so.

"No, I won't tell anyone. And thank you, Contessa."

I left her then.

As I started down the passage, Paul Duvall emerged from the stairway and walked toward me. With slightly malicious amusement I reflected that even though he had access to the Contessa's bedroom, apparently he was barred from her brother's elevator. Perhaps, though, he considered stair-climbing a way to keep that muscled litheness of his, in a place that offered neither polo nor water skiing nor even tennis.

We exchanged cool good mornings. As I entered the stairwell I looked back. He was tapping lightly on the Contessa's door. I went on down the stairs and along the corridor. When I reached the doorway to the courtyard, I looked out.

The red Triumph still stood on the cobblestones.

11

I FOUND THE boys sitting on the floor. Spread around them were windup cars and trucks they'd taken from the toy chest. Steven asked, "Well, do we get it?"

"Get what?"

"TV. And a new radio."

"I'm afraid not. Your uncle doesn't consider radio and TV suitable here. And he's right. Whoever heard of TV in a castle?"

He opened his mouth. Afraid he was going to ask whoever heard of air conditioning in a castle, I hurried on, "It's only for a little while. And we'll find other things to do. For instance, I saw lots of small stones out on the mesa. If we could get some sort of mortar, we could build our own castle."

Their faces lit up. Then Steven said accusingly, "I suppose he'd want to be in on it, and you'd let him."

"Mr. Carstairs? He'll be gone." Surely his presence wouldn't be tolerated much longer. Where was he now? Still having his arm dressed?

"His car's down there."

"I know. But he won't stay." Surely,

though, he'd contrive to say goodbye to me, and arrange for our meeting again soon.

Tommy asked, "He won't ever come back, will he?"

A tap on the door saved me from having to answer. "That'll be Juanita, with lunch. Steven, Tommy, gather up those toys."

When Juanita had set down the luncheon tray and left, there was still a fire truck on the floor. As I restored it to the chest, I noticed the case which contained a child's phonograph and half a dozen records. The phonograph had been his mother's Christmas gift to them, Steven had told me, when he was five.

"Who needs radio?" I asked, hauling out the case.

Thus we lunched to "Jingle Bells," "God Rest Ye Merry," and "Rudolph the Red-nosed Reindeer." Pleased by the music and the thought of Len's imminent departure, my two charges passed from sullenness to near-boisterousness.

When Juanita had removed the dishes, I walked over to the window. Behind me, Tommy asked, "Can we start building the castle now?"

"No," I said dully. "Lessons first."

The red sports car wasn't down there.

He'd left without seeing me, or even tapping the horn in farewell. Or, if he had, I hadn't heard it because of the phonograph music.

The boys were protesting loudly. Why couldn't they, for just once, Steven asked in martyred tones, have lessons afterward?

I turned. "Because you can't!" Then I softened my expression. It wasn't right to take it out on them. "But we don't have to stay up here. We can take our lessons down to that terrace on the west side of the castle."

We did. While Tommy frowned over his multiplication table, and Steven, with a re-signed air, did long division problems, I stared out over the juniper-dotted mesa. Why hadn't he said goodbye? He could at least have sent a note by one of the servants. But although I'd spent a good fifteen minutes gathering up books and papers and pencils, and tightening a not-very-loose button on Tommy's shirt, no note had arrived.

After they'd finished their arithmetic, I drilled them in spelling, both English and Spanish. At last I said, "That's all for now."

"Are we going to begin on the castle?"

"No, Tommy." I couldn't work up the requisite enthusiasm. "I'll have to try to get something to hold the stones together, and I don't feel like doing it today."

Seeing their crestfallen faces I added, "But you could start gathering stones. Pile them up out there where we played softball."

They raced off. For perhaps half an hour I watched them scurrying about, first near the pitcher's box, and then, as pickings grew lean, farther afield. At last, deciding they'd worked long enough under the hot sun, I strolled over to the sizable heap of stones. The boys ran up to me, panting. "That's a wonderful start. You can add to it tomorrow."

Tommy dropped two stones onto the pile, and then brushed his palms together in a workmanlike gesture. "I found another one. It didn't trip me though."

"Trip you? Oh, you mean another pipe in the ground. Where?"

He pointed to a clump of juniper about thirty feet west of the one where he'd taken a tumble that morning. "How many pipes do you think they put out there?"

"I don't know, dear. Maybe I could find out." I doubted, though, that anyone at the castle could tell me. The pitted metal of the pipe I'd seen that morning must have been exposed for decades to wind-driven sand and pebbles.

We walked back to the castle. As we

entered the courtyard, a faint, irrational hope died. He hadn't returned. We entered the lower corridor, and then started up the stairs, with the boys in the lead.

Nurse Walmsey, white-clad and majestic, appeared at the top of the stairs and began her descent. When only four or five steps separated us she said, "I'd like to speak to you, Miss Haversham."

"Of course. Boys, go to your room and wait for me, please."

When they'd disappeared she descended three more steps and then stopped, looming tall above me. "I've just put Mr. Carstairs in the room two doors from Steven's and Thomas's."

I said, after a moment, "Would you mind repeating that? I'm afraid I didn't quite—"

"I told you that I have put Mr. Carstairs—"

"Mr. Carstairs!"

"—in the room two doors from the children's room. The intervening room is unfurnished. Several of the rooms along that corridor, it seems, are unfurnished. Mr. Hind told me to assign him a room, and when I went to the housekeeper, she said to give him—"

"Mr. Hind!"

"—that room. Yes, Miss Haversham, Mr. Hind has invited him to stay until he feels well enough to travel. Mr. Hind is generosity itself, and therefore is often imposed upon. I believe he is being imposed upon now. There is something odd about your friend's wound, Miss Haversham, very odd."

"Odd!" I said, and realized I'd begun to sound like an echo.

"Miss Haversham, pretend I have a knife. I am about to stab you in the throat or face. Now protect yourself." She loomed closer above me. Involuntarily I shrank back, and almost lost my balance.

"What?"

"I am trying to prove something. Throw up your arm to protect your face. Quickly, Miss Haversham."

She was so large, and the space was so narrow, and her voice so peremptory, that I actually felt a thrill of alarm. I crooked my arm and held it before my face.

Her forefinger, stabbing out, traced a line along my arm. "Exactly."

"Exac—?" Irritated with myself, I amended, "What do you mean?"

"You exposed the underside of your arm to the knife," she said triumphantly. "Any-

113

one would. Now where is the wound on Mr. Carstairs' forearm?"

"The outside," I said reluctantly.

"Exactly. Therefore my belief is that the wound was self-inflicted. At least, it was not obtained in the manner he described. Incidentally, the cut was superficial, although he seems to regard himself as gravely wounded."

Self-inflicted. Was he so desperate to see me again that he'd slashed his arm in order to gain admittance here? I wasn't fatuous enough to believe that.

He'd been making a fool of me.

I said in a flat voice, "Have you told Mr. Hind?"

"Certainly not! Mr. Hind has been my patient for many years. He has high blood pressure, and it climbed several points this morning after he was obliged to admit . . . that journalist. And after all he's suffered at the hands of journalists. No, Miss Haversham, you and your . . . admirer can rest easy on that point."

She was shrewd in some ways, but not in all. Len Carstairs wasn't my admirer. If he'd used a ruse to get in here, it had been for some other purpose than to gain another sight of my gladsome face and lissome form.

"But my sense of professional dignity," she went on, "makes me want you to know that he didn't deceive *me*. Good day, Miss Haversham."

"Good day." I flattened myself against the wall. She flattened herself against the other wall, sidled past me, and then, turning, went down the stairs with majestic tread.

She's in love with him, I thought. Probably she didn't know it, but she was in love with the cripple in her care.

12

WHEN I REACHED the second floor landing, I saw that the first door along the corridor stood open. After a moment's hesitation, I moved purposefully to the doorway.

"Hello!" he said.

Shoes off, he sat with legs stretched out on the bed's yellow coverlet, back and head propped against a plump pillow. Despite the gauze bandage covering his left forearm, he looked fit enough to wrestle alligators.

Beside him on a night table stood an almost empty glass of orange juice. When he saw me look at it, he said delicately, "It's to help me regain my strength. A beautiful girl with long black braids brought it to me." He paused. "Well, aren't you going to come in and cheer me up?"

"I think I will," I said grimly.

I marched in, moved a straight chair near him, and sat down. A swift glance around showed me that the room was about the size of mine, and just as well furnished. Like mine, it contained a flat-topped walnut desk of modern design, practical for its purpose however inappropriate to its surroundings. He had a private bath, too. I could see it through a partially opened door.

He saw me looking at his bandaged arm. "The Abominable Snowwoman took five stitches," he explained. "Say, is that practicing medicine without a license? Are nurses authorized to stitch a wound?"

"I wouldn't know." I paused. "Pretend I have a knife. Throw up your arm to protect your throat and face."

"What is this? Some kind of game?"

"Go ahead. Do it."

After a moment he raised his right arm, palm turned inward. Gray eyes regarding me over the top of his forearm he asked, "Do I win? Is this what you mean?"

"I suppose so." As he took his arm down

I added, "Most people do it differently. The inside of the arm would be exposed."

"Well, I'm a very different sort of fellow."

"You sure are," I thought. Aloud I said, "Miss Walmsey thinks you're lying about that cut. She thinks you got it some other way."

He pursed his lips. "Does she now? I thought she seemed a bit fishy-eyed. Well, I suppose I could go out and try to round up that fellow who slashed me. But it seems like an awful lot of trouble, especially since she probably wouldn't believe him either, even if I could get him to admit it."

For a moment I was silent. Then I asked, "Where's your car?"

"Someone drove it into the garage."

I'd never thought of that possibility. But then, I'd had no reason to. I'd assumed he'd be hustled off the premises as soon as his arm was dressed. I never dreamed to see him here, lounging on a bed with a glass of orange juice beside him—orange juice served by "a beautiful girl with long black braids—"

I asked acidly, "How long will you be confined to your bed of pain?"

"Oh, I'll get up tomorrow."

"I suppose you'll be leaving then."

"No, Max Hind has invited me to stay as long as I want to."

"*What?*"

" 'Struth. Ask Miss Walmsey. She was just finishing up with my arm when a flunky came in and said Mr. Hind wanted to see me. She and I crossed the courtyard to that big room, the one that looks like something out of Versailles, and there he was in his wheelchair. We chatted for a while—he's really sort of a nice guy, do you know?— and then he said I could stay here as long as I felt like it. I think I'll stay at least a week."

For a few more dumbfounded moments I stared at his bland face. Then I rose. "I must be getting back to the boys."

"Be seeing you," he said, as I turned toward the door.

Not turning back, I said, "I suppose so."

I found the boys cold-eyed and accusatory. "He's still here!" Steven said the moment I entered. "We looked out in the hall because you were gone so long, and we heard you talking to him."

"I know. And I'm afraid he's going to stay awhile."

For perhaps ten seconds they were silent, staring at me. Then Tommy let out a crow. "You don't like him anymore!"

"I never did." Two pairs of eyes looked at me, undeceived. "I mean," I floundered, "I didn't like him a great deal."

Steven said, all magnanimity now, "Oh, he's not so bad. I guess he was pretty brave, taking that robber's knife away. But I guess girls don't appresherate things like that."

"A-pre-she-ate. I guess girls don't. Now why don't you two take a nap? You've had an active day."

Steven said, "I'm too old for naps."

"Well, I'm not. And I'm tired. Will you boys play quietly for an hour or so?"

Happy and docile now, they assured me they would.

I crossed the bath to my room, closed the door, and took off my shoes and dress. Even though I'd come in here to think rather than sleep, I did feel tired. In my slip, I lay down on the bed and stared at the ceiling.

Why had Max Hind told Len he could stay? Because he'd taken a liking to him? It was hard to imagine Max Hind liking any journalist. Why, then, had he wanted Len to stay?

Probably for the same reason he hadn't wanted Juanita to leave, even for a day. And now I was absolutely sure that his reason, whatever it was, had nothing to do with a hepatitis outbreak. Once Len had been sent upon his way, he might have contracted hepatitis—if there was such an epidemic—and carried it somewhere else, but he wouldn't have brought it back here.

No, Max Hind had some other reason for contriving that Len, once he was inside, remain here.

Len must have thought he'd won the chess game, so to speak, the two of them had played down there in that luxurious drawing room. His ruse—the slashed arm, the threat to tell the world of Max Hind's callous treatment of a wounded man—had not only gained him admittance. A surprisingly affable Max Hind had invited him to stay.

But maybe he hadn't won. Maybe he wasn't Max Hind's guest. Maybe, like the rest of us, he was—

My mind seemed to stop working for a moment.

Then I thought, "Get out of here. Take the boys and get out."

A moment later, aware with irritation of my panic-quickened heartbeats, I told myself sharply, "Stop being an idiot!" Where had it come from, that impulse to snatch up the boys and run, as if from some dark and howling doom soon to close in about this place? True, Max Hind was eccentric, unpredictable, and high-handed. But was that any reason for the fine hairs on my arms to stand up, as they had a moment ago?

Still, I told myself, it might be interesting—just as a sort of mental game—to consider means of taking the boys away, in the highly unlikely event that such a course became advisable.

Could we leave on foot? Scarcely. Even if we could somehow make our way unchallenged through the inner and outer gates, and past the guards down there, I couldn't lead the boys, especially Tommy, over the fifteen desolate miles to the nearest village.

Steal a car from the garage? That might be possible. Difficult, but possible. Perhaps, catching any bystanders by surprise, we might drive across the courtyard, through the entrance to the passageway, and then bypass the guards by swerving out onto the mesa's hard-packed earth for a hundred feet or so. Surely the guards wouldn't shoot at a car which held Max Hind's nephews.

Then I realized it was quite impossible. Someone would pursue us. Even if the pursuer never caught up, Max Hind would long since have picked up a phone in those well-guarded quarters of his and alerted the police in towns for miles around. It would end with me in custody, and the boys, shocked and frightened, back at Castle Estillio.

But it didn't matter, because no such attempt to leave would become necessary. As I'd already concluded, the presence of Julia Ascoli and Paul Duvall ruled out the possibility of any sort of dangerous situation here. Besides, Julia Ascoli had assured me —and her words had carried conviction— that the boys were quite safe.

That panicky impulse of a few minutes before must have been caused by sheer tiredness. Perhaps I'd better nap, after all. I closed my eyes.

Len, pulling a trick like that—probably so that he could sneak material for an exclusive story on Castle Estillio and its peculiar owner. How contemptible of him to pretend he'd followed *me* up here.

Don't think about him. Sleep. Sleep.

Finally I did.

13

A TAP ON the bathroom door awoke me. Tommy called,

"Juanita's brought our supper."

Hastily I washed the sleep from my eyes and combed my hair. When I entered the next room, I found Juanita transferring covered dishes from the tray on the serving cart to the table.

"Next I take a tray to Mr. Carstairs," she said brightly. "Is handsome man, no?" She giggled at some recollection. "And so *fonny.*"

"As a rubber crutch."

"*Perdón?*"

"Just an American expression." Maybe she was beautiful, rather than just pretty. How wretched to discover that I didn't like the idea of her being beautiful.

Damn that man.

After supper I played jackstraws with the boys, losing badly to both of them. Their baths after that, and then bed.

I went to bed too. But perhaps because of my nap that afternoon, I couldn't sleep. For a while I read Mr. Josiah Ward of Boston, but soon his unflagging good spirits irritated me past endurance.

When I'd been down in the library the evening before, I'd glanced through an eighteenth-century book, *Strong Points and Fortifications.* With its old-style spelling and page-long sentences, it wouldn't be easy reading, but then, its very difficulty might put me to sleep.

Should I go down in my robe? No, it was still early, not yet eleven. I might encounter someone. And it wouldn't look well for the boys' governess to be prowling around in her nightgown and robe. I got out of bed and began to dress.

When I entered the library from the corridor door, I was glad I'd bothered to dress. The Contessa was in the drawing room, talking to someone. Through the closed double doors I couldn't distinguish individual words. All I could hear was her voice, interspersed with her occasional hearty laugh, and answered now and then by the rumble of a masculine voice.

Crouching, I searched the Castle Estillio shelf. The book I'd come for wasn't there.

Had Paul taken it, hoping it might help him find whatever he sought here? I doubted that. I'd never seen him read anything, not even a newspaper. I couldn't imagine his plowing through a book filled with obsolete words, and s's that looked like f's. Julia Ascoli would never have looked into such a book. Her brother might have, but I doubted it. From all I'd heard, he was interested only in scientific subjects. And it seemed unlikely that any of the servants, few of them English-speaking and perhaps many of them illiterate, should have taken the book.

That left Len Carstairs. Well, maybe he'd been given permission to use the library, just as I had.

For a few minutes more I scanned the shelves. Finding nothing that appealed to me, I left the library and climbed to the second floor.

As I started past Len's closed door, I hesitated. If he had taken *Strong Points and Fortifications* from the library, perhaps he'd finished with it by now.

I knocked. Somewhere on the other side of the door, a metal object crashed against wood. Then there was silence.

Uneasily I stood there, waiting for the sound of his footsteps. Could it be that, despite his healthy appearance, he really had lost quite a lot of blood. Perhaps he'd started to get up from his bed or chair to answer my knock, and then fainted.

The knob turned under my hand. As the door swung back, something furry shot out into the corridor, brushing against my leg. I gave a startled little cry, and then realized it was the big orange cat I'd seen in the courtyard that morning. Streaking along the corridor through the bluish neon glow, he turned and disappeared down the stairs.

I pushed the door farther open, and saw what had made the metallic sound. A student lamp on the flat-topped desk lay, still burning, on its side. The cat must have made his way along some projecting ledge, through that open window, and onto the desk. Perhaps he'd been toying with the lamp cord when my knock sent him hurtling to the floor.

I looked around the room, aware of the odd shadows cast by the upward-striking light. The bed was empty. No sound came from the bathroom, its door standing wide open. Obviously Mr. Carstairs wasn't in.

Moving forward to right the lamp, I halted. The cat's alarmed leap had displaced something else. On the floor, face up, lay a sheaf of eight-by-ten photographs, held together at one corner by a metal clip. Bending, I picked them up. As I straightened, light played over the shiny surface of the top one, obscuring its subject. I reached out to place the sheaf on the desk, and then stood frozen with shock, arm half-extended.

I could see the top photo clearly now. It

was of a girl. She was dead. And she'd died violently.

Perhaps, when alive, she'd been pretty. The long blond hair spread out over a dirty carpet—the camera had revealed the spots clearly—hinted at attractiveness. So did the sprawled slender body in its torn remnants of slacks and a light-colored blouse. But the sash cord wound tight around her neck had done disfiguring things to her face . . .

In the grip of a sick fascination, I lifted the top photo. The second was also of a woman, lying half on, half off, a studio couch. She'd been older and heavier, but her strangulated face appeared no more and no less grotesque than the girl's.

I didn't look at the others. I just stood there, the sheaf of thin cardboard in my numb hand, and stared at the elongated shadow of a chairback on the opposite wall. At first only my stomach had reacted, tightening with cold nausea. But now my mind began to fumble with questions.

Why did he have such photographs?

Oh, he could explain easily how he'd obtained them. All large newspapers have such pictures in their files, pictures they'd neither desire nor dare to publish, pictures snapped by police as their first step in the investigation of violent death.

But what sort of reporter, what sort of *man*, carried such pictures with him on his vacation? What sort of man had sat here sometime earlier this evening, looking at the picture of that girl . . .

That girl who'd probably been about my age.

My thoughts came to a dead halt for a moment, and then moved on.

Until late this afternoon, I'd believed that he'd followed me to Castle Estillio. Could I have been right about that?

And the photos themselves. This morning I'd seen a camera, an expensive one, in the well behind the Triumph's bucket seats. He'd moved it aside to make room for Steven.

Perhaps the police hadn't taken those photographs. Perhaps in an apartment's improvised darkroom in Paris or London or some other city, the man who'd been the last to see that girl alive had hung over a stainless steel tray, thin face intent in the dim red light, waiting for a pitifully sprawled body to take shape in the developing fluid . . .

No! I wouldn't let myself imagine such terrible things. At least until a few hours ago,

I'd liked him. He'd seemed pleasant, humorous, perfectly normal—"

"Do you think you should be looking at those?"

For a moment I stood rigid. Then I whirled around, dropping the photos. He stood well inside the doorway. Light from the fallen lamp cast his shadow, enormously tall, on the wall behind him.

He walked toward me. I didn't move. But everything inside me shrank away from him.

Stooping, he picked up the photos, carried them to the other side of the desk, and placed them in a drawer. The faint click of its catch sounded loud in the stillness. He looked at me through the oddly slanted light, a waiting expression in his eyes.

I heard my own thin voice. "There was —a noise in here. I thought you might be ill. I opened the door, and a cat ran out. He'd knocked over the lamp, and those— those—"

"I see." His motions deliberate, he straightened the lamp, adjusted its shade. "You must have wondered about those photos. They're from newspaper files. A Czech psychiatrist I interviewed a few months back asked me to collect such pictures for him. He's writing a book. You know, *The Psy-*

chopathology of Violence, or something like that. He has a theory that the . . . methods used by various criminals indicate their particular mental quirks. His name's Carl Mallek. Maybe you've heard of him."

Two years before, a Dr. Carl Mallek had given a series of lectures at the Sorbonne. Since he was fairly young, and indisputably handsome—tall, with flaming red hair—his lectures had been especially popular with the girl students.

I said, after a long moment, "Yes, I think he was a guest lecturer at the Sorbonne. An elderly man, walks with a limp?"

He shook his head. "You must be thinking of some other Mallek. The one I know is a red-haired man, about thirty-five. I wrote him a few weeks ago that I intended to spend a few days in Prague during my vacation, and would bring him some photos."

Some of the tension left me. At least he did know Carl Mallek. And yet something in his words, his manner, hadn't rung true.

"Thing is," he was saying, "that I haven't typed the identifying flimsies to paste at the bottom of the photos. I'll get around to that tomorrow."

After a moment I said, "With your injured arm?"

He smiled. "I think it will be all right by tomorrow. And I'm sorry you saw those photos. If I'd had any idea you'd come in here —I mean, they must have given you quite a turn."

"They did, rather."

He let the silence lengthen. "Well, good night," I said awkwardly.

"Good night."

I went down the corridor. With my hand on the doorknob of my room, I hesitated, reluctant to shut myself in with the thought of long blond hair fanned out over a dirty carpet. Turning, I moved across to one of the window embrasures, pushed the narrow panes apart, and looked down.

Apparently someone was still in the drawing room, because light from its windows shone out onto the narrow ledge which, that morning, had brought me vicarious giddiness. There was light from another source too, slanting in a broad beam from above down onto the plain. I thrust my head out as far as possible through the narrow opening but still couldn't see the window from which the light fell. To judge by its slant, though, it came from the northeastern round tower.

Had Max Hind converted it into some sort of study? Perhaps.

Going into my room, I looked at the thumblatch on my door for a moment, then turned it. I undressed, got into bed, and opened Josiah Ward's book. Now his corny cheerfulness was welcome to me. It acted as a counterirritant to my chill, lingering unease over those moments in Len Carstairs' room. At last, when the hands of my clock pointed to a few minutes past one, I turned out the lamp. Then, wanting more air, I crossed to my casement window and pushed the panes wide apart.

The courtyard floodlights had been turned off. The night seemed utterly silent. And yet someone besides me was awake. A light, dulled by grimy windowpanes, shone briefly from a third floor room of the service quadrangle. It went out, only to come on again for a few seconds. So, unable to find what he sought on this side, Paul had moved to the storerooms opposite.

For an interval the third floor across the courtyard was dark. Then the light reappeared, about twenty feet farther east. He'd moved on to the next room . . .

Below me, light suddenly fanned out into the courtyard. A man ran out onto the cobblestones, then turned to face the entrance to the lower corridor and the drawing room. I heard the Contessa's laughing protest. "You wretch! Bring back my necklace."

He held it up. Pearls, lustrous even from up here. "Come get it! And pay for it."

Julia Ascoli, in silver lamé pants and a dark top, came out to the courtyard. The two figures merged. After a moment, taking her shoulders, he turned her around, fastened the necklace in place, and kissed the back of her neck.

Apparently neck-kissing was a standard part of the Duvall technique. Well, it wasn't to be sneered at. For perhaps more years than he'd care to acknowledge, it had brought him the sweet life.

Then I stiffened with realization. It wasn't Paul Duvall up there in those storerooms.

The two below had gone back inside. The light on the cobblestones narrowed, then disappeared as the drawing room door closed. I waited. So, too, did the searcher, who must have been alarmed by that sudden burst of light and sound. After about five minutes that dull gleam again appeared briefly, from about the same location as before.

Who was up there?

And where had Len Carstairs been when

I found his room empty? He'd volunteered no explanation of his absence, and, until now, I hadn't thought to wonder at it. Had there been a flashlight projecting from his hip pocket when he returned to his room? I hadn't noticed one. But then, I'd been too upset to observe closely.

I called my thoughts sternly to order. I wasn't going to believe it was he, moving with flashlight in hand behind those grimy windowpanes. Probably it was some servant assigned to night watchman duties. And I was going to accept his explanation about those photographs. It was a reasonable one. Perhaps the odd constraint in his voice as he gave it had been only an embarrassed reaction to the all-too-apparent suspicion in my own manner.

In short, my sense of justice demanded that I believe him.

Then, as the light shone again briefly, I forced myself to admit that it wasn't only my sense of justice which was involved. It was also my self-esteem. I didn't want to think that, even for the space of an hour spent at a sunny sidewalk table, I'd been attracted to a man who was evil.

Turning, I went back to bed.

14

THE NEXT MORNING I awoke with no memory of bad dreams. Perhaps I'd had them, though, because even before I opened my eyes I was aware of that vague sense of oppression which often follows a night of troubled dreaming.

After breakfast I assigned Steven a theme on Sir Francis Drake, and handed Tommy a list of words, all of which he habitually misspelled, with instructions to copy each one four times. Returning to my room, I mended a broken shoulder strap on one of my slips. Then, too restless to sit quietly and do my other mending, I went out into the corridor, opening and closing the door softly so as not to distract my laboring scholars.

I crossed the corridor, noticing as I did so that Len Carstairs' door was closed. For a few minutes I looked out at the plain, stretching away to the north from the mesa's base. Through the air I could see, in the distance, a small cluster of dwellings. Juanita's village? Perhaps. It was in the right direction.

Turning, I moved to the western end of

the corridor and looked out over the mesa. Then, hearing the Contessa's voice, I brought my gaze back to the terrace directly below. At midmorning, the chairs and the table with its furled umbrella were still deep in shadow. The Contessa and her brother sat at the table, apparently enjoying the brief coolness before the sun climbed high.

I regarded the top of Max Hind's graying head. Len had described him as "sort of a nice guy." I too had found him so during my first and only interview with him, down at the villa a few days before. True, he'd made a dry reference to the *Life* article my father had written about him. But when, unwilling to apologize for my father in any way, I'd made a politely noncommittal answer, I'd seen a gleam of wry appreciation in the tired and embittered eyes behind the horn-rimmed glasses. Later, he'd asked a few questions about his nephews' progress, and seemed pleased and surprised by my answers.

Yes, I'd rather liked him, and had thought he rather liked me. But apparently he didn't now. His voice, growing louder at the end of a sentence, sent the words "damned Haversham girl" floating up to me.

I didn't catch his sister's reply, but apparently she pointed out that he'd approved of me, and considered me bright, because he said forcefully, "Too damned bright. Asking you all those questions. That's why I wanted you to leave her in San Ysidro."

"I *told* you." As always when her ire was aroused, the Contessa's voice had grown loud. "She's been the only one who can manage those two. Anyway, if you'd taken them to live with you in England—"

"Their place was with you! I'm too busy to be burdened with young children."

"Busy!" Her tone was contemptuous. "And what does it get you?"

When he finally replied, his voice held a dangerous edge. "I can't stop the rest of the world from saying such things, but by God I can stop you. I won't have my own sister, a sister I support, treating me as a laughingstock."

No doubt aware that she'd gone too far, she didn't answer. Fleetingly I thought of some of the public statements that had made Max Hind an object of ridicule. In 1962, for instance, he'd predicted—on the basis of similar seismic disturbances to those which had preceded the disaster of 1631—that Vesuvius would have a major eruption before the end of the year. There'd been no such eruption.

He was speaking again, still angrily, "And now that damned newspaperman has followed her up here. Well, if I'm wrong this time, he won't know about it. Nobody will. I've made sure of that."

The Contessa spoke soothingly. I caught a phrase here and there—"in a week," and "know one way or the other," and "able to leave here."

A week! Did she mean we were to stay here until only a week from now? She'd told me we might stay a month. Besides, if our residence here was to be so brief, why all those tons of food?

"—won't be shady much longer," I heard Max Hind say. "Do you want to call Kurt? Or can you manage?"

I didn't catch her reply. She started to rise. Afraid her gaze might wander up to the window, I stepped back out of the embrasure.

As I passed Len's closed door, I thought, "If Max Hind has decided to shorten our stay that much, at least I won't have to see *him* after next week."

Then, as I put my hand on the knob of the boys' door, another part of that conversation down on the terrace echoed in my mind. If he was wrong this time, the Contessa's brother had said, no one would know about it.

What scientific will-o'-the-wisp was he pursuing this time? What was he doing over there in his private quarters? Inventing a perpetual motion machine? Trying to develop a lawn grass that would grow to the height of one inch and then stop?

Well, probably I'd never know. As he'd told his sister, he'd made sure that no one would.

I found the boys still bent over their tasks. "Tell me when you're through," I said. Going into my room, I resumed my mending.

After a while Steven crossed the bath to my room. "We're finished."

I checked their work, making sure first that Tommy had copied each word four times, and then turning to Steven's theme. I read it through, marking one misspelled word and one sentence error. "Very good," I said. As a matter of fact, it was excellent. But Steven, unlike Tommy, couldn't take too much praise. It made him overconfident.

"Can you boys go out to the mesa alone? I haven't finished my sewing."

When they'd gone, I went back to my room and my accumulated mending. About fifteen minutes later I heard the door of the boys' room burst open. I crossed the bath to find Steven kneeling beside the open toy chest. "We need our ball and bat," he explained.

He rushed out. I went back to my sewing. Several minutes passed before I realized that it was strange that Steven had returned for the ball and bat. Yesterday both boys had been intent upon gathering stones for the castle. What had diverted their interest?

Getting out into the corridor, I moved rapidly to the window at its western end. Len was down there on the mesa. Holding the light bat in his right hand, he stood at home plate, about thirty feet from the neglected pile of stones. Behind him, Steven was sunk in a catcher's crouch. Tommy was on the mound, small hand clutching the ball, face contorted with concentration.

"Let me have it, Tommy boy." Len tapped the hard earth with the bat end. "Right here. Right over the plate."

Tommy pitched. The bat sent the ball racing past him. "Wow!" Steven said, straightening up. "And with only one hand."

"Wait'll he can use both hands!" Tommy screamed.

Hands. I thought of the blond girl, and of the sash cord someone's hands had tightened around her neck, until it bit deep into the flesh. I gripped the window ledge, hard. The children shouldn't be down there with—

No! I wasn't going to think such things. I'd settled that last night.

Still, I did have legitimate reason to resent his presence down there. I'd started the boys upon a project that would be educational, *creative*. And now, just because a not-too-ethical journalist could bat a ball with one hand . . .

My mending could wait. I went rapidly down the stairs, across the courtyard, and out onto the mesa.

Steven was at bat now, with Len pitching. Steven hit a fly ball. Lazily, Len reached up and caught it. "You see that?" Steven greeted me. "I betcha he could play in the big leagues."

"Not even in the minors," Len said modestly. His eyes were clear and direct in the sunlight, his smile warm. I found it almost impossible to believe that last night, as he'd moved toward me through the oddly angled lamplight, everything within me had shrunk away from him.

"Don't say 'betcha,' " I said, turning to Steven. "Say 'bet you.' Better yet, say 'I think.' "

Steven asked wonderingly, "What's the matter with you?"

"Nothing! I just thought you'd be gathering stones."

"We will, this afternoon. Right now Len's teaching us baseball."

"I taught you. I drew the diamond, and—"

"You didn't know what a passed ball was. It was in the baseball story I read, but you didn't know what it was."

"Or a wild pitch, either," said the younger of my perfidious charges.

Len ruffled the taffy-colored hair. "No woman ever understands baseball, Tommy."

"I do." My voice was cold. "When I was a little girl, I went with my grandfather to a baseball game every Saturday."

"But that was a long time ago," Steven said practically. "You've probably forgot a lot of it."

Catching my eyes, Len smiled. "Now Steven, let's not be ungallant."

Steven looked puzzled. "But it was a long time ago."

"Never mind," Len said, in an infuriatingly tactful tone. "I'll draw the diamond, and then I'll show you anything you want to know."

Having traced a diamond with his bat, he pantomimed a catcher fumbling a good pitch, and making a futile lunge at a bad one. After that, sometimes placing Steven and Tommy in the outfield or on the bases to help illustrate a point, he demonstrated the balk, the double play, and the technique of sliding into base to beat the throw. At last I intervened.

"That's enough racing around in the hot sun. Particularly for you," I said coldly to Len. "You're supposed to be a wounded man."

"That's true. But when you run across two fine little fellows like these, so obviously in need of masculine companionship—"

"Come, boys," I said. "It's almost time for lunch."

Although plainly reluctant, they accompanied me without spoken protest. And after we'd crossed the courtyard and entered the downstairs corridor, Tommy took my hand. "He's nice, but we still like you best."

I squeezed his hand. "Thank you."

"And," Steven said, "as soon as we've

finished our lessons this afternoon, we'll gather more rocks."

His tone was one of generous concession. "Well, never mind," I comforted myself. Once they actually started building the castle, they'd find it far more exciting than watching Len Carstairs hit an imaginary fly ball and then race to center field to put himself out.

They did gather more rocks that afternoon. I worked along with them. By five, when it was time to get ready for supper, the pile was almost as tall as Steven. As soon as I obtained some kind of mortar, we'd start building.

A minute or so after we'd returned to the boys' room, Tommy cried, "Where's my Snoopy? I've lost my Snoopy!" He meant his wrist watch, with Snoopy's picture on the dial.

Steven snorted. "Len has it. You broke the strap, remember, and he said he'd take care of it for you."

Tommy's face clouded with anxiety. "Maybe he broke it. He had it in his pocket, and he slid into that base—"

"I'm sure he didn't," I said swiftly. "And if he did, I'll see that you get another one. Now wait just a minute."

I went down the corridor and tapped on Len's door. "Come in, Juanita," he called.

I opened the door. He sat at the flat-topped desk, a small opened book before him. At sight of me, he got to his feet. "Oh! I thought you were Juanita, coming to take my dinner order."

I said, outraged, "Your dinner order! The boys and I take what's brought to us."

"Well, perhaps she feels that a man, especially a wounded one, needs nourishing fare."

I ignored that. "Do you have Tommy's watch?"

"Good lord!" He clapped his hand to his hip pocket and then drew the watch out. "For a minute I was afraid it was broken."

Advancing a couple of steps, I took the watch from his hand and placed it in my skirt pocket. My lowered gaze swept the book's outspread pages. The right-hand one bore an engraving. It was hard to be sure with the book upside down, but it looked like a geological cross section of a hill, with a rock strata slanting through it. No, the edges were too even to represent any sort of natural strata. I couldn't see the book's title, but from its small size, and the worn edges of the leather binding, and the fine, old-style printing on the left-hand page, I was sure it was Richard Hall's *Strong Points and Fortifications*, the book I'd sought in the library the night before.

He said quietly, "Dinah."

I raised my eyes to his. "Yes?"

"That day in San Ysidro I thought we were going to be friends. What's gone wrong? Is it those photographs? I know they're not pretty. But I explained why I had them. Don't you believe me?"

After a moment I said, "Yes, I believe you."

"Then what's wrong?"

I blurted out, "Just why did you come here?"

His gray eyes studied me. "If I told you I'd kept thinking about you, and finally decided there was no reason to wait until after my vacation before seeing you again—"

I just looked at him.

"So you won't buy that."

"No, I won't."

"Then why do you think I'm here?"

"Probably to get some sort of story on Max Hind."

"And that's so reprehensible? After all, I'm a reporter."

"So was my father. He wrote about many

famous and important people. But he never sneaked and lied to get a story. He never slashed his arm to blackmail his way into someone's private property!"

He flushed, whether with embarrassment or anger I couldn't be sure. But he didn't deny the charge. "Well, I'm not your father."

"You certainly aren't. Thanks for keeping Tommy's watch." I started for the door.

"Dinah." I turned. "I did like you," he said. "I do like you."

Those nice gray eyes of his. That slight, grave smile. It wouldn't be too hard to forgive him for the trick he'd pulled. I'd heard of journalists doing worse things when in pursuit of a news beat.

And I needed to confide to him, or to someone, about the uneasiness that had assailed me even before we'd driven into the courtyard of this place. What's more, I wanted to like him. I wanted to feel again, as I had that day in San Ysidro's little square, that he might turn out to be the answer to the question, "What shall I do with the rest of my life?"

The trouble was I had no reason, no reason whatsoever, to consider him trustworthy. "Well, goodbye," I said, and walked out.

147

15

IF AGAIN THAT night someone moved through the storerooms, I had no inkling of it. All that rock-toting had tired me so that not even my conflicting thoughts about Len could keep me awake. Before ten, I was sound asleep.

But when I awoke the next morning, almost the first thing I thought of was that outspread book on Len's desk. Closing my eyes, I tried to visualize that old engraving. It had showed a cross section of a hill, flat-topped and steepsided. There'd been a little protuberance above the hill's level top at one end of the cross section.

Not a protuberance. Castle Estillio. And not a hill. The mesa. Those slanting lines, then, must represent the centuries-old tunnel which, according to legend, had permitted the castle's defenders to move unseen to the mesa's base, and stage a surprise attack upon their enemies.

Getting out of bed, I picked up Josiah Ward's book and turned to the chapter which dealt with Castle Estillio. I reread his account of how he'd searched the cavernous fireplace for the hidden entrance to the tunnel, and had received only grimy palms for his pains.

If my surmise about that engraving was correct, that book on Len's desk must also contain an account of that tunnel, and the means of access to it from the kitchen. In fact, it probably carried a far more detailed description, since it was, to put it mildly, a more scholarly work than Mr. Ward's.

If Len Carstairs planned to investigate that kitchen, how did he propose to get in? The answer was simple. Charm. He'd charm Juanita into persuading some member of the kitchen staff to admit him. Well, if that mammoth fireplace was still there, I hoped that Mr. Carstairs too would gain nothing but grime and cobwebs.

Around nine-thirty, I saw how wrong I'd been. Len had chosen a far more direct method for gaining entrance to the kitchen.

I'd settled the boys to their lessons after breakfast, and returned to my own room. Glancing out of the window, I saw Len standing in the center of the courtyard. Hands thrust into the pockets of his gray flannels, he was surveying the western battlements with the complacent, leisurely air of someone who has booked the deluxe, six months' tour of Europe.

I heard the whisper of rubber tires over stone. Then Max Hind, with Kurt pushing his wheelchair, appeared below. As usual, no matter what the temperature, his torso above the blanketed legs was impeccably clad in a dark suit jacket.

Len had turned. Max Hind said, "Good morning, Mr. Carstairs."

"Good morning, sir." His tone was both easy and deferential.

"I've received word that you'd like to see the service section of the castle."

"If it's not too much trouble. I've always found that the kitchen and other workrooms in these old places give you the best idea of how people used to live."

"No trouble at all. I'll guide you myself, at least as far as I can. There's no elevator in that section. Incidentally, except for my and my sister's private quarters, you may look at any part of the castle you desire. You see, I always try to be nice to the press." He laughed. "Not that the press often reciprocates."

Len too laughed, but otherwise didn't answer. As the three men moved across the cobblestones, Max Hind's voice floated back to me. "I've modernized extensively in this section, of course, but I've tried to retain some of the more interesting original features. The eleventh-century fireplace is intact, and in one of the supply rooms you'll see the wine press the Carthusian monks used."

Kurt left the wheelchair to knock on the ancient double doors which, according to the chart in the corridor downstairs, led to the kitchen. The doors opened, and the three men went inside.

For sheer brass, I decided, it would be hard to find Len Carstairs' equal. Less than forty-eight hours after he'd made himself Max Hind's uninvited and unwelcome guest, he'd obtained something that neither the boys nor I had—the run of three fourths of the castle.

Then I again reflected, with a strange mixture of malicious satisfaction and unease, that perhaps he had no reason to congratulate himself on his cleverness. Max Hind, I was increasingly sure, had other motives than hospitable ones for keeping Len sufficiently entertained that he'd linger on here.

While the boys labored over their morning studies at their worktable, I drew up their assignments for that afternoon. At ten-thirty

Steven crossed the bath to my room. "Can we gather rocks now?"

"May we. Yes, you may go as soon as I've checked over your lessons. After that, I'll shampoo my hair. But I'll join you as soon as I can."

I'd had my hair cut quite short for the summer. Since it's also fine in texture, it took me less than half an hour to wash it, and then dry it with my electric hand dryer. Leaving my room, I walked along the corridor toward the stairs. At the corridor's end, I stepped into the embrasure and looked out.

Len was down there with the boys. All three were wielding tools—trowels, probably—that flashed in the sunlight. Scattered around them was various paraphernalia—a wheelbarrow, a bucket that probably held water, a mixing trough, and a tall bag of what was probably cement.

So he'd beat me to it. I'd intended to ask Juanita at lunch time to find out if whoever was in charge of such supplies would let us have some mortar. Turning, I went swiftly down the stairs.

As I approached over the hard-packed earth, Len stood up and said, "Hi." His smile was as friendly as if there'd never been the slightest tension between us. "Would you like to go to work? You don't need a union card. And I brought a trowel for you." He nodded toward the wheelbarrow.

I looked down at what they'd already constructed. Into a square of cement about two feet by two feet, they'd been pressing rounded stones. The square was less than half-covered. "What's that?"

"The courtyard. It has to be built first, of course."

Of course. But I probably wouldn't have thought of that, although Steven might have. Under my direction, we'd have built the four sides of the castle to about Tommy's height, and then found it almost impossible to lay the courtyard.

Hoping my chagrin didn't show, I asked, "How did you get the tools and cement?"

"They were in one of the supply rooms below the kitchen. I told the man in charge of the power plant—it's down there too— about this castle project, and asked him if I could have some cement and some tools. He sent someone to ask, and our host sent back word to let me have anything I wanted."

I tried not to sound too sarcastic. "You do get around, don't you?"

"Well, as I told Mr. Hind, whenever I'm

in one of these old places, I like to see where the day-to-day work was done."

"I hope you found it interesting."

"Very. The kitchen's so big that at least twenty people could work in there without getting into each other's way. At one end he's put in the latest equipment—huge freezers, infrared ovens, the works. But the other end looks as if it hasn't changed much for seven or eight hundred years. There's this mammoth fireplace, six feet high and maybe twice as deep. There are stone benches inside it. I suppose that was so the cooks could sit there all warm and cosy while they waited to give the roasting ox another turn."

Moving to the wheelbarrow, he picked up a trowel and held it out, handle toward me. "Want to go to work?"

The boys, I suddenly realized, were sitting back on their heels, eyes fixed anxiously on my face. Because they liked him, they wanted me to like him too.

"All right." I took the trowel.

By lunchtime, we'd finished the court-yard. As the four of us walked back across the mesa, Len said, "While you and the boys are at lessons this afternoon, I'll set up a form for the front wall and pour the cement. By the time you come out, the cement ought to be just right, firm enough to stand alone but soft enough that we can press rocks into it."

Tommy asked, "What's a form?"

"A sort of hollow wooden box you pour cement into. When the cement's dry, or nearly so, you take the box away, and there's your wall, or terrace, or whatever."

Steven, ever the purist, halted in his tracks. "But the castle wasn't built that way. The real one, I mean."

"Son, it would take us months and months to build even a small model of Castle Estillio, even if we had some way to cut the stones into squares, which we don't. This won't look exactly like Castle Estillio, but it will look like *a* castle. And even though we can't have windows, I've figured out an easy way to make that entrance passage in the front wall."

Mollified, Steven made no further protest.

When the boys and I went out onto the mesa in midafternoon, we found Len standing beside a narrow form about two feet long by four feet high. He said, looking pleased with himself, "I'm glad you're here. I was beginning to be afraid I would have to have the unveiling without you."

While the boys and I watched, he took a hammer from the wheelbarrow and tapped all over the wooden form, then carefully lifted it. There, firm but still damp, stood the castle's front wall, complete with entrance passageway.

"Before I poured the cement," he explained, "I bent a piece of aluminum into quonset shape and placed it at the bottom of the form. That made the tunnel. I'll chisel the aluminum out later, when the wall's really solid. But right now we'd better move fast. In about an hour the cement will be too dry."

We did move fast, Tommy and I pressing stones from the pile into the castle's façade, and Len and Steven working on the other side. After a while, I realized I was having a lot of fun. And certainly the boys were. While we worked, Len kept up a stream of jokes, riddles, and the sort of self-deprecating anecdotes children love to hear from adults. There was the time in the Austrian Alps, for instance, when he'd spent an entire day climbing to a lofty peak, shivered in his sleeping bag through a night of near-zero temperature, risen at dawn to set up his camera for a sunrise shot, and found he'd brought no film.

Listening to the boys' delighted laughter, I recalled his remark of the afternoon before about boys needing "masculine companion-ship." He'd said it to needle me, but it was true. The thought miffed me a little. On the whole, though, I was more pleased, and grateful to him, than jealous.

When he could be this nice, how could he also be a conniver—or perhaps something worse? But no. I'd resolved to forget those photographs.

By four-thirty we'd finished the castle's front quadrangle. "When you come out here tomorrow morning," Len said, "I'll have an-other wall ready for us to work on."

With Len trundling the wheelbarrow, we went back across the mesa. I was aware of feeling pleasantly tired, pleasantly sun-burned. I was also aware that I wouldn't have had half as good a time if Len hadn't been with us. We were only a few yards from the entrance passageway when Tommy, tugging at my hand, signaled for me to bend down. I did, and he whispered in my ear. "All right," I answered, after a mo-ment.

Straightening, I said to Len, "Would you like to have supper with the boys and me tonight?"

"Great," he said promptly. "What time? About six?"

"Yes. Unless," I said, my voice cooling, "you've already ordered dinner from Juanita. In that case, you might find our food too simple for your taste."

"Oh, I don't give my order to Juanita until five-thirty. I'll ask her to bring roast chicken for four. Okay?"

He smiled at me, obviously unabashed.

It was impossible not to smile back. At least I found it so. "Okay," I said.

16

IT WAS A lovely dinner. Getting into the spirit of the occasion, Juanita not only wangled for us roast chicken with savory dressing, but also string beans amandine, endive salad, and ice cream with frozen strawberries for dessert. Delighted with the festive atmosphere—"Jingle Bells" on the phonograph, and Len propounding riddles as he carved the chicken—she lingered smiling for several minutes after she served the meal, thus earning, perhaps, a reprimand from her superiors in the kitchen.

After dinner Len proposed that we play concentration. He made a brief trip to his room to get the cards, and then spread the deck out, face down, on the floor.

Concentration was a good choice. With their sharp and uncluttered memories, children are fiendishly good at that game. Again and again, after Len or I had failed to turn over a mate to the first card we'd picked up, Steven would pounce on the right card, and triumphantly add to his stack of matched pairs. Even Tommy was soon matching up cards with disconcerting ease.

Len and I were going down to defeat for the third time when I became aware of a growing chorus of voices in the courtyard below. We all moved to the window.

At least twenty people, the women in blue cotton skirts and blouses, the men in pants and shirts of similar cotton, stood down there on the cobblestones, some silent, some exclaiming, but all with faces turned up to the night sky. Each face was washed with a light far warmer than that of the arc lamp attached to the battlements. Moonlight? No, it was more warmly golden than any moonlight I'd ever seen. Besides, I had a vague impression that the moon was in its final quarter, and therefore not even above the horizon now. Still looking down, I saw Julia Ascoli and Paul Duvall emerge from the doorway almost directly below us. They too turned their faces toward the sky. I said, "What on earth—?"

"I think I know," Len answered. "It must be that new comet. Tonight it's supposed to be really spectacular for the first time."

"Comet?"

"Didn't you read about it? It's been in all the papers."

"Oh, of course. It's just that I hadn't read anything about it lately. We don't get newspapers up here. And for several days before we came here, I was too busy to more than glance at the headlines."

Steven and Tommy were already at the door. "Come *on*," Steven said.

We hurried down the stairs and along the lower corridor. Just before we stepped through the archway into the courtyard, I saw that Nurse Walmsey had joined the growing crowd. Taller than all but the tallest men, she stood with white-capped head tilted back, and large-featured face bathed in that warm light. The moment I emerged into the courtyard, I too looked up.

There it was. Its luminous head, which appeared at least half as large as a full moon, seemed directly above us. Its magnificent tails—five, six, *seven* of them—fanned out behind the head in shimmering veils of light, so thin that a few of the brighter stars shone through. How far did those streamers trail their filmy radiance across the night sky? Down here we had no way of telling, because the northern battlements cut off our view.

Tommy had slipped his hand into my left one. Steven, who seldom made such gestures, now clasped my right. I looked down at their faces, bathed in that radiance. They looked frightened, and no wonder. Not a few of the adults in this mostly silent crowd looked frightened too. And even though, as a teenager at an English secondary school, I'd learned at least something about comets as part of a general science course, and even though my grandparents had recounted for me their own vivid childhood memories of Halley's comet—even so, I too felt not just delight in the comet's beauty, but a touch of primitive awe.

Tommy asked, in the hushed, faraway tone of a frightened child, "Will it fall down?"

"No comet ever has," Len answered cheerfully. "And the world's seen thousands and thousands of them."

"Perhaps a few have," I almost corrected. In a *Holiday* article my father had once written about Arizona, he'd mentioned that scientists believe that the enormous crater in that state had been dug by the head of a comparatively small comet. Right now, though, with two apprehensive small boys clinging to my hands, was no time to display such information.

Instead I said, "Boys, we're so lucky. It isn't often that a comet approaches the earth at just the right angle to give us a good view of it. Millions of people pass their whole lifetimes without seeing anything like this."

Steven released my hand. He said, all bold excitement now, "Can't we go out onto the mesa? Boy, oh boy! There we'd really see it."

I looked at the locked gates barring the passageway. Turning to Len I asked, "Think you could do something about it? You seem to be the one with influence."

He frowned thoughtfully. "People might follow us. And I don't think our genial host would like having his staff scattered all over the mesa." His face cleared. "Anyway, I've got a better idea. Follow me."

Turning, he began to retrace his steps. I led the two boys, each still with craned neck, in his wake. On the second floor he stopped. "Let's go up to the round tower. There's a

162

trap door onto the roof. Or at least there should be."

The round tower. Those nasty stairs, only a few inches wider than my shoulders, spiraling up into blackness . . .

"The tower. Boy, oh boy," Steven said, and Tommy echoed, "Boy, oh boy."

"Can't you two use some other expression besides 'Boy, oh boy?' "

Steven looked interested. "Like what?"

All the delighted exclamations that came immediately to mind, from "Smashing!" to "Top-hole!" to "Goody!", seemed equally inappropriate. "Never mind." Then weakly, to Len: "All right. We'll try it."

We waited until he went to his room for a flashlight, and then followed him up to the dark third floor, with its smell of moldering carpets and tapestries seeping out from under the storeroom doors. The flashlight's beam showed the tower's door, and the foot of that ancient spiral of stone steps.

Len led the way, with Steven behind him, and then Tommy. Battling my claustrophobic conviction that soon I'd get stuck, unable either to advance or retreat, I brought up the rear. Centuries later, we emerged into a round room. By the flashlight's refracted glow, I saw the arrow slits in the encircling wall of rough stone, and a flight of perhaps a dozen stone steps leading up to a wooden trap door in the roof. The steps were about twenty-six inches wide. If there'd ever been metal handrails, they'd long since rusted away.

Perhaps once, too, there'd been a chain dangling from the trap door, to facilitate closing it from the inside. But if so it too had disappeared. In its place, fastened to an iron ring in the door and dangling almost to the floor, was a length of thin but strong-looking rope. The rope coil from which it had been cut stood near the foot of the stairs.

Len looked at the stairs doubtfully. "Think you can manage those, with nothing to hang onto?"

"Of course." Now that I'd escaped that spiral staircase, I felt brave as a lioness.

He handed me the flashlight. "Then I'll go to work on that trap door."

At the top of the stairs he struggled with what looked like solid oak planking, raising it eight inches or so, pausing to rest, and then forcing it upward another few inches. At last, with one mighty heave, he sent it back onto the rooftop. The impact sounded like a cannon shot, and I wondered nervously if anyone would come to investigate.

After all, even if Len wasn't out of bounds, the boys and I were. But apparently in that vast place, with its foot-thick walls, the sound was lost. Either that, or everyone was too absorbed in the celestial show to pay any attention.

With my flashlight pointing the way first Steven, then Tommy, scampered up those narrow steps, as unconcernedly as they used to climb the pretty curving stairs at the villa. Len's arms reached down, and lifted each boy in turn up into the darkness. I climbed the steps rapidly too, careful not to look down on either side. Len helped me out onto the tower's roof. I switched off the flashlight.

Up here, with no competition from flickering matches or glowing cigarettes, the beautiful visitor appeared in all its glory. Back from its head, with the five glowing spots I knew must be the nuclei, the tails streamed almost to the horizon.

Although predominantly pale blue, those filmy streamers, with here and there a star showing through, also pulsed with other colors—green and yellow and red and violet—as the aurora borealis does, as a prism does in the sunlight. And, like the aurora, those streamers gave an impression of quivering, ever-shifting motion, as if they were tumbling hollow cylinders of luminosity.

The lovely thing made no sound, of course. And yet in my mind's ear I heard a singing, crystal-pure and indescribably sweet.

I felt Len's gaze on my face. "I know. It makes you wish there was some word stronger than beautiful. Just the same, you can see why comets used to scare hell out of people."

Tommy asked, "How does it just hang there?"

"It doesn't dear. It's moving, very fast. The reason it doesn't seem to is that it's so very far away."

"How fast does it move?"

"Oh, hundreds and hundreds of miles an hour." Glancing at Len, I saw his lips quirk, and realized I'd made a gross understatement.

"How high is it?"

"Oh, very high." I wouldn't be caught again.

Steven asked, "Was it there last night?"

A remembered bit of information from that general science course drew me onto firmer ground. "Yes, but perhaps it was still only a patch of light then, something you might not even have noticed if you hadn't known it was there. But as the comet moves closer to the sun, the bright spot or spots in the head—they're called nuclei—start to glow. And they begin to give off energy, in the form of those streamers."

I hoped he wouldn't ask me why. He didn't. "How long will it stay?"

"Why—why, I have no idea."

"We'll see it for five days," Len said, "according to what I read in the paper last week. For three days it will grow brighter, then it will start dimming, and then it will be gone."

Tommy cried, "Why can't it stay?" No fear in him now, just sorrow at the thought of beauty vanished.

"Because it can't, dear, any more than Christmas can stay, or spring."

"Will it ever come back?"

"Probably, but a long, long time from now." Surely that was right. If this was a "new" comet, then any previous visits to the earth's vicinity must have occurred before records of comets were kept. On such an orbit, it might be many thousands of years before this particular comet again displayed itself to the eyes of men.

"What's its name?" Tommy asked.

"Why, I don't know. Comets are named

after the person who discovers them." I turned to Len. "Do you know its name?"

"I read it, but I've forgotten."

"I think I know it," Steven said. "Its name is McGrath."

"Why, Steven! How on earth—?"

"I heard it on my radio when we were almost up to the castle. A boy in Scotland had found a new comet. His name is Donald McGrath. He's thirteen."

I remembered the broadcast then, vaguely. So a little Scots boy with a homemade telescope—I hoped it was homemade —had been the first to spot a hazy patch of light in the heavens. What must he be feeling now, as he saw his comet spread out to awe and delight the earth's millions.

"What makes a comet?" Tommy asked.

"I just don't know. Do you know, Len?"

He shook his head.

"Tomorrow we'll try to learn more about comets." Surely there were books on astronomy in the library. "But right now it's past your bedtime."

The boys, from whom I'd come to expect a minimum amount of bedtime grumbling, set up a vigorous protest, particularly Tommy. We stayed about ten minutes more, gazing at the Scots boy's comet. Then we descended those railless stairs, Len going first, and shining the flashlight up for Tommy, and Steven, and finally me to descend ("We'll leave the trap door open," he said. "It never rains this time of year. Besides, we'll want to go up there tomorrow night.")

Much later, after I'd put the boys to bed, and when I too lay in bed, staring at the warm light that fell past my casement windows into the now-silent courtyard, I thought, "What a lovely day!" Working on the miniature castle, with the smell of sun-warmed juniper and sage in my nostrils, and Len's gray eyes, after some joke had sent the boys into gales of laughter, smiling into mine. That festive dinner. And, finally, the most fabulous, the most beautiful skyrocket anyone could conceive of, quivering across the heavens for our delight.

I think I must still have been smiling as I fell asleep.

17

THE NEXT TWO days were equally wonderful. In the hours of hot sunlight, there was the smell of the mesa's sparse vegetation, and the boys' excited chatter, and Len's thin, gray-eyed face smiling at me over the walls of our miniature castle. By night, McGrath's comet shimmered and pulsed in the starry sky. Perhaps it's true that when falling in love one turns a bit daft. Anyway, the little Scots boy's comet still seemed to sing to me.

On the morning after that first night on the round tower, I went down to the library. All but one of its books on astronomy were either too outdated and fanciful for my purpose (*Heavenly Signs, Portents, and Divers Fantastik Wonders*, by James Mercer, 1672) or too abstruse (*Space, Time, and Gravitation*, by Sir Arthur Eddington, 1920). The exception was *Handbook of the Heavens*, by Hubert Bernhard, Dorothy Bennet, and Hugh Rice, 1952. On the flyleaf, written in a boyish hand, was the name Nicholas Lapidus. Evidently, when the Greek shipping tycoon owned the castle, some young member of his family was interested in astronomy. Perhaps, like the McGrath boy, he'd had his own telescope, and had taken it out onto the mesa at night. Certainly the clear dry air of this place would offer excellent viewing.

Before I left the library, I checked to see if Len had returned *Strong Points and For-*

tifications to its shelf. He had. Later I'd look into it. Right then, I was too interested in the comet. Somehow—and I suppose this indicates that I'd turned not only daft but appallingly egotistical—that glorious comet seemed a magic symbol of what was happening to me.

I suspended regular lessons that morning so that the boys and I could devote ourselves to the astronomy book. From it we learned that comets behave more whimsically than any other bodies visible in the heavens. While the major planets, including ours, move sedately in almost circular orbits, comets venture out on elliptical paths, some so far that they may leave our solar system entirely and become captives of some other sun, perhaps terrifying or delighting men who live on some planet circling that sun. Of those that do stay bound to our solar system, one comet, which visited us in 1864, was estimated to have an orbit of two million years. ("That means, boys, that when that comet was here time before last, only the ancestors of men were on earth, creatures who couldn't read, or write, or maybe even speak.") On the other hand, another comet stays so cozily close to the sun that we can see it as a hazy patch in the sky every three and a third years.

Whenever a comet comes within two hundred and fifty million miles of the sun, it speeds up enormously, attaining an ultimate velocity, relative to the earth, of thousands of miles each hour. (No wonder Len had smiled.) It is then that the coma, or luminous head, grows bright, and the nucleus begins to glow. Perhaps because of the radiation pressure of the sun, material is forced back from the coma to form the tail, or tails.

To Tommy's dismay, we learned that the comet we'd seen the night before was not the most spectacular ever to appear. In 146 B.C. a comet shone as brightly as the sun. The Great Comet of 1843 had a tail two hundred million miles in length. A comet in 1882 had eight glowing spots in its head, compared to five in our comet. And Borelli's comet of 1903 had nine tails.

Later that morning, out on the mesa, as I pressed a brown stone streaked with white into the castle's third wall, I looked up at Len and said, "I just thought of something. Isn't there a radio in your car?"

"I thought of that right after breakfast, and went down to the garage. The radio sounded pretty weak the last time I tried it, the day before I came up here, and now it's completely conked out. I thought of asking if someone here had spare parts for a transistor, but considering the way Max Hind feels about radios, I decided I'd better not."

Conked out. Of course it had. I didn't want to think of other possibilities. Not now. I just wanted to enjoy the sun's warmth on my back, and Tommy's crow of delight as he found a handsome red stone in the rapidly diminishing pile, and the sight of Len's deft, strong hands cementing into place one of the pointed bits of shale we'd selected to form the castle's jagged battlements. In short, I wanted to enjoy being happier than I could ever remember being.

The four of us again had dinner together, and afterward made the ascent through the narrow circular staircase and up the railless steps to the round tower's roof. The five glowing spots in the comet's head were definitely brighter now, and nearer orange than golden yellow.

"It's bigger," Tommy said happily. I think he hoped, despite what Len had said, and despite all we'd read that morning, that its apparent increase in size meant it might become a permanent fixture.

"That's because it's closer," Len said. "If I remember what the papers said last week, it will come still closer tomorrow. We may even be able to see it in the daytime. Then it will start moving away."

Tommy didn't argue—he was a naturally polite little boy, much more so than Steven—but I sensed his stubborn hope that the whole adult world was wrong, and that he'd always be able to see that glory streaming across the night sky.

When we went out onto the mesa the next afternoon we saw that the comet was visible. Oh, not the shimmering iridescent tails. They were lost in the bright sunlight. But we could see the head, glowing almost as brightly as Venus on a clear night.

Despite the distraction of that second, smaller sun in the sky, we finished the castle that afternoon, even the four round towers. To form the cement for those, we'd used small cans, obtained by Len from the kitchen, which had once held orange juice concentrate. Those cans had been my inspiration. Although the idea of building a castle had originated with me, those cans represented my only contribution toward solving our construction problems, and I was darned proud of them.

For a while we admired the castle, viewing it from all sides. Then Steven said, "I wish we were just starting on it."

I knew what he meant. The pride of accomplishment didn't equal the fun we'd had these past few days.

"Oh, it's not finished yet," Len said. "There'll be the moat. Castle Estillio must have had one once. Ours will still have. I'll cement the bottom of the moat so it will hold water. Then we'll build the drawbridge, and open and close it with string wound around a little pulley. And we'll build a portcullis for the entrance. Soon ours will look more like a real castle than your uncle's."

All the way back across the mesa, and later on through dinner, we discussed construction plans, enlarging them to include an outer wall beyond the moat. But when we stepped through the trap door onto the roof, we no longer said much of anything. We just looked.

As if in gala farewell, the celestial visitor appeared lovelier than ever, the luminous head with its five glowing eyes brighter, the color pulsations of the filmy tails so rapid that even as you saw a glow of violet or emerald it had turned to yellow or white. Mainly for Tommy's sake, I permitted our staying up there to a scandalously late hour, almost ten-thirty. When we finally turned to the trap door, I glanced at that bulbous-topped northeastern tower. As on the other two nights we'd been up here, no light shone from it.

We descended to our corridor. Accompanying us to the door of the boys' room, Len said, "Get a good night's sleep, gang. We'll want to work hard tomorrow."

He looked at me, and his smile took on another quality. "Good night, Dinah," he said softly. "Pleasant dreams."

For a while after I'd put the boys to bed, it seemed that I wasn't to dream at all. I felt as wide-awake as if it were high noon. I turned my bedside lamp on again, and began to read Josiah Ward. For a while, each time my thoughts began to stray, I jerked them back to the book. But after about an hour I suddenly realized I'd read three pages without absorbing a word. I'd been too busy entertaining a fantasy in which Len and I sailed back to America on an ocean liner, something I'd never done, and waited for the ship's hold to disgorge the red Triumph, and then drove to Wisconsin, to see his parents and that tree he'd fallen out of, and then drove on to North Dakota to see my grand-parents . . .

Well, if I couldn't concentrate on my reading, I might as well have another look at the comet.

Slipping on a robe, I went quietly across the corridor and into the embrasure opposite my room. I leaned far out of the window so that the neon glow behind me wouldn't hamper my vision, and then looked up. All I could see from there were the ends of three shimmering streamers. I'd been prepared to find them already dimming. But they still pulsed with iridescence. Like a great and gracious lady of the theater, the comet seemed reluctant to start withdrawing from a still-enthusiastic audience.

I stood there for perhaps five minutes, and then stepped back out of the embrasure and turned around.

The door of Len's room was opening. I stood stock-still as Juanita emerged. She was smiling. For a moment she paused, thrusting a small roll of bills down the neck of her blouse.

She took two steps, saw me, and stood as still as I did. For a moment we stared at each other through the neon glow. Then her face turned scarlet. I saw that even her throat and

bosom blushed, down to the point where her
V-necked blouse concealed her grandmother's crucifix, and the roll of bills. Head lowered now, she hurried past me to her room.

Cold and sick, I went into my own room
and closed the door.

18

NOT TAKING OFF my robe, I lay down on the
bed. With the dreary regularity of a dripping
faucet, my mind repeated, "Fool, fool,
fool."

I'd known he was no sterling character.
(Like the touch of a bat's wing, memory
brushed me. Those hideous photographs I'd
found on the floor in his room.)

And yet, because of his smile, and because
I'd liked him in San Ysidro, and because he
seemed good for the boys, and because of
the sun's warmth on the mesa, and because
he'd appeared to take pleasure in building
the castle, and because we'd stood beside
each other in the dark with glory streaming
across the heavens, and—oh, for a dozen
silly reasons, I'd let myself pretend he was
all I wanted him to be.

Was tonight their first assignation? Or had

the affair started almost as soon as he arrived here? Had he, each night she served dinner to the four of us, sent her a silent message over my head? Probably, probably.

Through my pain and jealousy and humiliation, I felt a surge of outrage on Juanita's behalf. He knew as well as I did that in this part of the world a maiden's loss of virtue was still a serious, even calamitous, matter. And I was sure she was—or had been—virtuous. There was a young man in her village whom she'd intended to marry. They'd have married before this, except that his family—as impoverished as hers, and much more numerous—needed all the money he could make raising sheep on a few arid acres. But, she'd told me, her dark eyes soft and her dimples showing, they'd find a way to marry soon.

And now . . .

How could I have fallen in love with a man like Len Carstairs? How *could* I? Well, I'd just have to live through it. I'd told Tommy that wonderful things like spring and Christmas and that lovely comet can't stay forever. Neither did the first fierce onslaught of pain last forever. I'd found that out in the months since that schooner had capsized in the Caribbean.

There was a light tap at the door.

Thankful that my face was unmarked by tears—perhaps later I'd find the release of weeping—I moved to the door and asked, "Who is it?"

"It is Juanita."

After a moment I opened the door. She'd been crying. Her brown eyes were reddened, her cheeks slightly swollen. I said in a curt voice, "Come in."

Closing the door behind her, I turned and said, "Well?"

"Oh, Dinah!" She'd never called me that before. "It is that I know what you thinked." She lapsed into Spanish. "But it is not true, not true! I think of you as a friend of my heart. And you must believe. I am a good girl!" She clasped her hands a few inches below her quivering chin.

I said, merciless as the headmistress of a Victorian young ladies' seminary, "Good girls aren't seen coming out of a man's room at this time of night—with a roll of bills."

"But it was for this that he gave me the money!" Diving into the pocket of her blue cotton skirt, she brought up a manila envelope and held it out to me. It trembled slightly. Wonderingly, I took it and reached inside.

A sheaf of prints. Color prints of paintings, about a dozen of them. Two looked vaguely familiar, although whether I'd seen the originals in some gallery or museum, or merely reproductions, I had no idea. However, I recognized the styles and periods of all of them. That bearded man and that bent old woman might be Titians. This Descent from the Cross, with the greenish cast to the body of the dead Christ, and the grief-ravaged faces of the women mourners, might be an El Greco. Two were definitely of the Raphael school, although not necessarily by him. And there were several that looked to be pre-Renaissance Italian—Giottos, perhaps.

I said slowly, placing the prints back in the envelope, "I don't understand." I gave her the envelope, and she thrust it back into her pocket.

"I am to look for them." With a childlike change of mood, she seemed excited now, even proud. "In the storerooms, over there." She pointed toward the forbidden eastern quadrangle.

"Why? Why should he pay you to—"

"It is for his article. He is a journalist, no? And he is writing about Mr. Hind, no? To write that these paintings are here will give him a good . . . crook to his story."

"I imagine he said angle." Although crook, I reflected bitterly, hadn't been an inappropriate word. "Did he say why you're finding these pictures might give him a good angle?"

"No, but he knows. He is a journalist."

Did she actually believe he was in search of an "angle"? Looking into her guileless face, I saw that she did.

The searcher that first night, who almost certainly was Paul Duvall. The searcher the second night, who most certainly wasn't. Duvall and Carstairs, two cats of the same stripe, prowling after the same mouse. And a very fat mouse. If those paintings were what they appeared to be, lesser works of several Old Masters, they must be worth millions. No wonder Paul Duvall had been eager to undergo weeks of boredom up here. No wonder Len Carstairs had been willing to slash his own arm to gain admittance.

Another possible reason for his presence crossed my mind, but I flung rather than thrust it aside. I wasn't going to be self-deluded twice.

I said sternly, "If there are such paintings here, they must belong to Mr. Hind." I'd never heard, though, that he was interested in the arts, either major or minor. Down in San Ysidro, for instance, Julia Ascoli had told me that her brother had placed the furnishing of the castle's drawing room and family rooms in the hands of a decorator, one that she had chosen for him.

"What difference if they are Mr. Hind's? Mr. Carstairs wants to know about them only for his angle."

"Juanita, you mustn't do it. You'll get caught, and then you'll be dismissed."

"Why should I care? I am rich!" She drew the rolls of currency from the neck of her blouse. "Look at this."

I unrolled the bills. They were few in number, but high in denomination. To Julia Ascoli, this sum might mean only a daytime frock from a Paris couturière. To Juanita, it must represent about half a year's salary.

"And there will be more if I find the paintings. Enrique will have the money to start the petrol station. I will take charge of it whenever he must tend the sheep." I'd heard before about the station. Tourist traffic through her village was increasing. If her sweetheart could lease a roadside site, and a pump from the petrol company, he'd be able both to support his present family and to start a new one.

She was smiling, lost in some dream of a shiny red pump, petrol-needy tourists, and a *niño* in her arms for the tourists to exclaim over.

I handed the money back to her. "There's no way for you to get over there except past the guard on the first floor. Surely there's a guard at night, too."

"The guard at night is Carlos." She giggled. "I have told you about him."

She had, one day at lunchtime. Carlos was a homely man, very homely. He was in love with her. And after he came off duty each morning he drank, "until sometimes he fall down." At that point in her narration, Tommy had begun to reel about the room, crying, "Look at me, look at me! I'm drunk!" I'd shaken my head at Juanita, and sternly ordered Tommy to come to the table.

Now she said, "If I must, I will give him this." She held up a bill, one of the lowest denomination. "But I think that without the money he will let me pass. To have a girl smile at him, a man so ugly will do anything."

Our sex too, I had to admit, can be pretty unprincipled in pursuit of its goals—the

184

husband, the secure household, the happy and healthy child. "Juanita, don't get mixed up in this. He wants to steal those paintings. They're valuable. You could end up in prison. Believe me."

Her eyes grew round. "Mr. Carstairs? A thief?" Then her expression softened to amused understanding. "I have seen you look at him. I know how you feel. You must not care that he asks me to help him with his article, and not you. It is only that it will be easy for me to search."

She thought I was merely jealous. She was *sorry* for me. I said, abandoning all attempt at argument, "When are you going to try?"

"Tomorrow night, after midnight. Do not worry. It will be easy for me."

I said vaguely, "All right." Suddenly I felt exhausted. "We'd both better try to sleep now."

After she'd gone, I lay awake in the darkness. Should I tell Max Hind, or the Contessa? No, I decided. If I put them on the alert for Len Carstairs, they might soon discover that other night prowler. And then, to Julia Ascoli, I'd be like the messenger of ancient days bringing bad news to the oriental potentate. She wouldn't have me beheaded, but she'd fire me.

Staying with the boys was the important thing, more important than ever now. If I didn't want to risk leaving them alone, I'd have to let Len continue his devious way, and Juanita her headstrong one.

I stayed awake for another half hour or so, and then fell into exhausted sleep.

19

AFTER I'D SETTLED the boys at their lessons the next morning, I slipped down the corridor to Len's door. Through the heavy wood I could hear the click-click of his typewriter. I knocked.

"Hi," he said, a moment after he opened the door. Then his face altered. "What is it?"

"May I speak to you?"

He stepped back for me to enter the room, and then closed the door behind me. I said, "I came to ask you to have nothing more to do with the boys."

"What-a-at?" His eyes registered puzzled astonishment, but a second before I'd seen a sudden alertness there.

"You're not a fit companion for them. I know what you're up to. And what's even worse, somehow, I know you've bribed Juanita to help you."

He looked not only alarmed now, but angry. "So she told you."

"She felt she had to. I saw her coming out of your room last night. I don't suppose you'd understand," I said coldly, "but a girl like Juanita couldn't let anyone think—what I did think."

He turned to the window. Back turned, he said, with equal coldness, "I suppose you've told Max Hind or his sister."

"Not yet. But can you think of any good reason why I shouldn't?" Let him suffer for a minute or so.

He turned around. "I don't know whether or not you'll consider it a good reason, but —you might get me killed."

"Paul Duvall?"

He nodded. The quizzical look in his eyes told me he wondered how I knew.

"You needn't worry. I'll keep quiet. Oh, not to save your skin. I have urgent reasons of my own for not getting mixed up in this."

"The boys?" His voice was quiet.

"The boys. I mustn't risk getting fired." I put my hand on the doorknob. "Well, that's all I came to tell you. Stay away fror them."

He looked tired now, and sounded tired. "Whatever you say."

I went back to my own room. At ten-thirty, bracing myself, I crossed through the bath to break the bad news.

"Steven, Tommy." Seated at the study table, they turned to look at me. "Mr. Carstairs won't be helping us with the castle after this. In fact, you're to have nothing more to do with him."

Astonishment in the small faces. Then Tommy said sorrowfully, "You're mad at him again."

"If you want to put it that way. But he isn't—a suitable person. You may speak to him if you chance to meet, but that's all. I mean it."

Steven rose, walked over to the toy chest, and kicked it. Ordinarily I wouldn't have stood for that. But remembering the fun we'd had out on the mesa, I felt he should be allowed that one kick. "No moat," he said.

"No little bridge," Tommy mourned. "No little bridge with a string. We were going to pull the string, and the bridge would go up and down—"

"Maybe there'll be no bridge, but we can

still have the moat. I'll get some cement, so we can make it hold water."

"Len already had cement." Steven's voice was sullen. "And he was going to make a pencil sharpener into a winch for the bridge, and—"

"Steven, that'll be enough!" My head ached, and I felt the pressure of tears behind my eyes. "You're to have nothing more to do with Mr. Carstairs."

He looked somewhat cowed, and yet stubbornness lingered in his face. After a moment he ventured, "Why?"

I, who'd always tried to explain my decisions to them, fell back upon the traditional reply of the sore-beset adult. "Because I say so. Now let's go down to the courtyard. I'll try to get you something to dig with. Then you can go out onto the mesa."

Tommy asked, "Aren't you coming with us?"

"Not this morning, nor this afternoon, probably. I have a headache." Besides, in my present mood, it was better that I supervise them from afar. I could keep checking from the window at the western end of the corridor. "Perhaps tomorrow I'll help you."

Looking unhappy but resigned, they accompanied me down to the courtyard. A stout woman, carrying a two-handled wicker basket piled high with ironed sheets, was emerging from the laundry. I hurried toward her.

"The young gentlemen need something to dig with. Small shovels, if they're available. Will you please see if you can get them for us?"

Setting down the basket, she went back to the laundry. The boys and I waited in the cool shadow of the castle's eastern quadrangle. Was Len watching us from his window? I was sure of it. I could almost feel his gaze.

A manservant emerged from the kitchen, two garden trowels in his hands. Would these do? I assured him they would. The curved steel blades looked stout to penetrate the mesa's soil. But as I handed them to the boys, I saw discontent in the face of my little classicist, Steven. What castle ever had a moat dug with a silly garden trowel?

They disappeared through the shadowy passageway, and I returned to my room. All that morning I kept going down the corridor to the western window. They were digging, all right, but even from that distance their motions appeared half-hearted.

When they came back for lunch Tommy announced, "It's still there." His tone seemed to add, "At least that's something." After a moment I realized he must mean he could still see the comet.

"Of course it's still there. Le—The newspapers said it would be visible for a few more days. But it won't stay."

Wonderful things never lasted.

Then, touched by his disconsolate face, I added, "But you'll see another comet."

"When?"

I wasn't sure just when Halley's comet was due to return. Sometime in the middle nineteen eighties, though. "Not too long from now. You won't even be fully grown. And it's a fine comet. My grandparents saw it when they weren't much older than you are now."

When the boys returned to the mesa late that afternoon, I again kept checking on them from the western window. In all those trips down the corridor, I didn't encounter Len, or hear the click of his typewriter from behind his closed door.

At supper that night we played "Jingle Bells" three times. I told jokes I'd dredged from memory during that long day, jokes which as a small child I'd found hilarious.

The boys tried to respond. Evidently, fine kids that they were, they'd decided between themselves that Dinah was unhappy, and that they should be nice to her. But still, there were long minutes during which only the phonograph music broke the room's silence.

Damn that man.

But at least Juanita was happy. As at lunchtime, she seemed to fill the room with a joyful glow when she came to serve our supper. Aider and abettor of criminal enterprise though she was, I found myself hoping she'd get away with it. If Juanita ever stood beside that petrol pump, cradling her firstborn in one arm while she unhooked the hose with the other hand, Len would have added a little to the world's happiness, however inadvertently.

There was no rooftop viewing that night, of course. Alone, I'd never have dared shepherd the boys up and down those railless steps. But I did allow them to cross the corridor, where Steven stood in one window embrasure, and Tommy, standing on the phonograph case, looked out the window next to it. I kept my door open, so that, as I mended the sagging hem of a plaid skirt, I could look up and make sure that they didn't manage to lean too far out of those narrow apertures. I myself didn't even want to look at the comet. If it hadn't been for the exhilarating effect of that visitor flaunting itself across the sky, I might not have made a fool of myself.

They'd been out in the corridor only about a minute when Tommy came back to complain that now he could see only "one little-bitty piece" of one tail. I told him that I was sorry, but it was the corridor or nothing. I didn't want them going down to join the courtyard crowd—a crowd much smaller than on the first night of the comet's appearance—nor did I want to accompany them. I might encounter Max Hind or the Contessa, which would make me feel guilty, or Len Carstairs, which would intensify all I was feeling already. Furthermore, I didn't relish the idea of standing half an hour or so at the dangerously wide window above the courtyard, clutching the waistband of a small boy in each hand.

At last I crossed the corridor and told the boys it was bedtime. When they were settled for the night, I returned to my room. Trying to tire myself sufficiently to sleep, I washed out some stockings, and straightened bureau drawers. By eleven-thirty, I'd drawn the draperies against the comet's glow, gone to bed, and turned out the light.

Soon Juanita would be slipping down the stairs and along the corridor to the family quarters. Had she already made her arrangement with the "so homely" Carlos? Probably. And would he open any storeroom doors she might find locked? Perhaps. In her headlong pursuit of that petrol pump, she wouldn't hesitate to dazzle the poor man into complete befuddlement.

I turned over in bed and resolutely told myself to sleep.

A soft but urgent sound. For a few seconds it was a flicker, who'd suddenly appeared to peck at one of the trees in the Wisconsin woodland—somehow I knew it was Wisconsin—where I wandered beside a vaguely familiar blond man. Then it was someone knocking at the door.

I switched on the lamp. Twenty of two, by my bedside clock. Sleepily I called, "Who's there?"

"It is Juanita." Even through the door, I could hear the terror in her voice.

Wide awake now, I picked up my blue chenille robe from a chairback and struggled into it. I opened the door, and she slipped quickly inside. She wore a cheap black coat over her blue skirt and blouse. A black rayon scarf, knotted under the chin, covered her hair. In contrast to the black material, her face was as white as death.

"Juanita, what on earth's happened? Why are you—"

"Shut the door! Please, please!"

I shut it. Her pupils were so distended that her brown eyes looked black. "I am to run away. To my village, tonight. I have the suitcase packed—"

"Juanita! Speak Spanish. Why are you running away? And how can you, tonight? The gates are locked and—"

"I shall take sheets from one of the supply closets." She spoke in Spanish, with breathless haste. "There is a vacant room above the kitchen. I shall knot the sheets together, and climb out the window—"

"One of those outside windows? They're too narrow. It would be hard for anyone larger than Steven to get through."

"I must try! I must be with my mother and sister and Enrique. I must! Oh, Dinah! If you have any family, try to get to them."

I said, bewildered, "I have no one." No one except the boys. "I've told you that. Now will you try to explain what frightened you? Take it step by step. You went over there"—I pointed toward the east—"and Carlos let you pass, and then what? Now try to speak slowly."

She did try. Drawing a deep breath, she said, "The storerooms were all unlocked. In them I found no pictures, and no crates that might hold pictures. Mr. Carstairs had told me to look for crates. Then I tried the door to the tower over there, and it was locked—"

Abandoning her effort at calm, she made a wild verbal leap. "And then it wasn't locked, and I went inside, and there was one of those machines they have in office cinemas, and I heard—Oh, Dinah!"

She began to cry, the tears pouring unchecked down her contorted face. "It is terrible, terrible! I must go now. I must be with my mother and sister—"

She started toward the door. "Juanita, please!" I caught her by the shoulders. Her unexplained terror had begun to infect me now, so that my voice rose. "Can't you get hold of—"

Someone knocked. I stood motionless for a moment. Then I turned and asked, "Who is it?"

"It is Kurt, Miss Haversham."

I opened the door. Even now, in the morning's small hours, he'd dressed with German correctness in his uniform. He gave me that slight, governess-sized bow, and then looked past me to Juanita. "Come with me. The Contessa needs you."

I turned to look at her. She appeared terrified, but no more so than before. In fact, I felt she hadn't even heard him.

I asked sharply, "Why should the Contessa want Juanita? She has her personal maid."

"Elena becomes ill at the sight of blood." His voice held faint contempt. "The Contessa has had an accident. She slipped in the bathroom and cut her head on the basin. Mr. Hind's nurse has bound the wound, but she feels she must stay with Mr. Hind, who is very upset. That is why the Contessa has sent for Juanita."

It was impossible to be sure whether or not he was telling the truth. I rather thought, though, that he was. He had the air of a man repeating a message exactly as he had received it.

In a quandary, I looked at Juanita's fear-dazed eyes. Should I go to the Contessa in her place? No, that wouldn't do. Left alone, Juanita might try to carry out her wild scheme of wriggling through one of those narrow windows and letting herself down to the hard ground two stories below. What was more, the Contessa, already upset by her accident, might be angry indeed if I, rather than Juanita, came to sit beside her.

Kurt said, "Come. Don't keep the Contessa waiting."

Apparently his words had at last gotten through to her. "The Contessa!" Eagerness mingled strangely with the fear in her eyes. "She will understand. She will see to it that I get to my village."

She moved swiftly into the corridor. I stood in my doorway, watching the thick-necked chauffeur and the slender girl in the cheap black coat move past Len's closed door and then turn to descend the stairs.

For at least half an hour my tired mind fumbled with questions. Should I have let her go? And what had she seen—no, heard, she'd said—to put her in that incoherent state? Something that had seemed to her supernatural? Although of at least average intelligence, she'd had very little education to modify her peasant background, with its centuries-old superstitions. Keyed up as she must have been as she searched through those forbidden rooms, she might very well have heard something which convinced her that an invincible menace moved through these stone corridors. Surely that must be it, since her terror had been for me as well as herself.

But why had she said, "If you have any family, try to go to them"? What would my family, supposing I'd had one, have to do with it?

I shouldn't have let her go over there in that hysterical state. Julia Ascoli, upset by her accident and perhaps in pain, would have no patience with the girl. But perhaps that would be all to the good. Perhaps, just to get rid of her, the Contessa would disregard her brother's wishes and send Juanita to her village.

My mind gave up then, and I slid into sleep—only to be awakened not too long afterward. I don't know how long, because I didn't rouse myself sufficiently to turn on the light and look at the clock. It was a sound from overhead which had awakened me, the muffled, metallic clangor of some object rolling across a stone floor.

Paul Duvall searching up there? Len Carstairs? Well, let him. I didn't care. Turning face down, I slid my arms around the pillow and was almost instantly asleep.

20

NOT ENTIRELY TO my surprise, another maid brought breakfast to the boys and me the next morning. She was a plump woman of about thirty, with a coarse-featured but pleasant face.

I asked in Spanish, "Where's Juanita?"

"In the kitchen someone was saying that she went to her village last night."

Tommy asked, "Isn't she coming back?" He was fond of Juanita, who'd always taken care of him and Steven at the villa on my days off.

Poor Tommy. Of late he seemed destined to lose everything precious to him—his comet, and Len Carstairs, and the prospect of his little-bitty bridge worked with string —and now Juanita.

"I think she'll be back," I comforted. "She was just homesick. Grownups too get homesick, you know."

Two hours later, when they'd finished their lessons, I said, "Well, shall we go down and try to get cement for the moat?"

The boys exchanged glances. Then Steven said politely, "We're sort of tired of working on the castle. We'd like to play with the trains today."

I understood. Compared to the dazzling plans Len had outlined, the prospect of building just a moat, with no drawbridge, and no portcullis, seemed unexciting. Well, that was only natural. It took more years than either of them possessed to learn to settle, with good grace, for second best. "All right. We'll set out the tracks."

Around eleven, closing the door on the rattle of speeding trains, I moved down the corridor to the embrasured window at its end. I stared out at our castle, standing behind its partially dug moat.

Why, I wondered, does any abandoned toy—a sand fort crumbling on a late-September beach, a battered doll at the roadside, even a teddy bear in an attic trunk—hold such pathos? Is it that such toys seem to symbolize the childhood that, perforce, we abandoned?

I heard the sound of an opening door. Turning, I saw Len emerge from his room. He said, "I was just coming to see you." He hesitated. "Would you come in for a few minutes? I'd like to talk to you."

I asked evenly, "Can't we talk here?"

"All right," he said after a moment. He

walked to where I stood beside the window. "It's about Juanita."

"She went to her village. I suppose the Contessa arranged for it."

He nodded. "The maid who brought my breakfast told me that was where she'd gone. But it seems strange she'd leave without—" He broke off.

"Without reporting on what you'd bribed her to do? She didn't report, and she didn't give the money back. Is that what's upset you?"

He flushed. After a moment he said, "It doesn't seem to occur to you that I might be worried about the girl herself. You must take a pretty dim view of me."

"Oh, I thought that was obvious." Then, in spite of myself, and although I was sure I had no reason to, I felt a stab of compunction. "But maybe you really are worried about her. If so, I apologize. As for the money, I'm sure she'll send it back to you."

"Did you see her at all last night?"

"Yes." I told him about her hysterical visit to my room, and of her eager departure with Kurt.

"You have no idea who frightened her?"

"No, but I got the impression it was *something,* rather than someone. My guess is that she was afraid of something . . . supernatural. She was so hysterical that I made scarcely any sense at all out of what she said."

"And you think the Contessa, out of sheer exasperation, just packed her off?"

"Yes. The Contessa has a very low exasperation point."

He frowned. "I suppose you're right. Still, I think I'll send a note over to Max Hind at lunchtime."

"Asking about Juanita? That sounds like a good idea." I paused. "Well, is there anything else?"

"Yes. How are Steven and Tommy?"

I said coolly, "They're fine. I'd better get them ready for lunch now." I nodded to him, and walked away.

When afternoon lessons were over, I said, "You boys had better get some fresh air. If you don't want to work on the moat, why don't we play ball?"

"Couldn't we stay here?" Tommy asked. "We could build things with the erector set."

How disappointed they must be, if they didn't even want to go near our castle. "All right," I said.

Dinner that night again was rather subdued. For a while afterward Steven and I took turns reading aloud from *The Wind in the Willows*. Then, with less protest than usual, the boys went to bed.

Around ten someone knocked at my door. I opened it to find Len standing there. "I thought you might want to see this," he said, and handed me a note. "I'd have brought it earlier, except that it seemed best to wait until the boys were in bed."

I unfolded the single sheet of paper. The note read:

Dear Mr. Carstairs,

I'm sorry that I can't see you. My sister suffered a slight accident last night, and that brought on one of my spells of high blood pressure. My nurse, Miss Walmsey, forbids me to see anyone.

As for Juanita, my driver took her to her village last night. She seemed to be suffering from some sort of hysterical attack. All we could get out of her was that she wanted to return to her mother and sister.

I hope that the maid who has taken her place is satisfactory, and that you are still enjoying your stay with us.

It was signed, "Max Hind."

I said, handing the note back to him, "Well?"

"It's just that I didn't hear any car drive out or return. And I was awake most of the night."

Awake doing what? Waiting for Juanita to report? Prowling through the floor above this one? "Perhaps there's another garage. After all, there's a branch road leading around to the eastern side of the castle."

Relief came into his face. Perhaps, I reflected, he really had been concerned about her. He said, "I remember now." He looked at me for a moment. When I didn't speak, he said, "Well, good night," and turned away.

Closing the door, I sat down on the bed. In spite of what I'd said to Len, I myself didn't feel reassured. True, there might be another garage, but it seemed unlikely. The garage off the courtyard was large enough to house that whole fleet of station wagons and the two limousines, with space left over.

After an indecisive moment, I went out into the corridor and walked past the intervening room to what had been Juanita's door. The knob turned under my hand. I groped for the switch, pressed it. The room sprang into view. A width only about half that of my room. Serviceable carpeting of brown cotton. A narrow metal bed, a chest of drawers, a straight chair, and a washstand.

I looked into the closet first. Empty. Then I searched the chest of drawers. Also empty. She must have come back here after she'd gone over there with Kurt, packed her things . . .

No, that was wrong. When she came to my room, she'd said she'd already packed her suitcase.

She'd been afraid someone might prevent her leaving. She'd even been ready to make a dangerous escape out a window. Would she, then, have left her suitcase in plain sight when she came to me? Perhaps, but more probably she'd have taken the precaution of hiding it, in case someone came looking for her—as, indeed, Kurt had come looking.

I knelt on the floor, lifted the white cotton spread, and looked under the bed. No suitcase.

Getting to my feet, I stood motionless for a moment. There was that vacant room next to this one. Perhaps, on her way from her room to mine . . .

Turning off the light, I went out into the corridor and opened the first door to the left.

When I pressed the light switch, I saw that furniture had been moved into this room, but not arranged. It stood in the middle of the floor, the narrow bedstead leaning against a bureau, and the straight chair shoved against one side of it.

I walked around the pile of furniture. There on the floor was the scuffed cardboard suitcase, secured by two hempen straps buckled around it, which she'd brought from San Ysidro. I stared at it, feeling a tightness in the pit of my stomach.

To the poor, even the least possession is precious, and that suitcase probably held everything Juanita owned. No matter how frightened, she would never have left without it.

She was still here.

21

"FIND HER," I thought, aware of my quickened pulsebeats. But how? The whole eastern side of the quadrangle was inaccessible to me. And alone, I'd find even searching the other three sides an enormous task. There was only one person to help me, and

I had little reason to trust him. But I'd have to trust him, at least in this.

Turning out the light, I closed the door softly, hurried past my room and the boys, and tapped on Len's door. A few seconds later, it opened.

"Oh!" he said. Then, sharply: "What's happened?"

"I'd better come in."

"Of course." He opened the door wider, and then closed it behind me.

Standing in the middle of the room, I told him about the suitcase. "There's no use going to Max Hind or his sister about it. They'd just lie."

He nodded. His face was pale.

I managed to get the words out. "I think she's dead."

Again he nodded. "I've had that feeling all day, or at least ever since you told me she was supposed to have left in a car."

He hadn't heard a car, although he'd been awake most of the night . . .

That sound that had awakened me, sometime before daylight. That muffled, metallic rolling, as if someone's foot had struck the heavy casque of that fake suit of armor.

I asked, again aware of that sick tightening

in the pit of my stomach, "Were you on the third floor last night?"

Startled alertness came into his eyes. He must be wondering, I realized, when I'd first become aware of his searching late at night. But all he said was, "No."

"Someone was up there." I added with reluctance, "There's a long chest in one of the rooms. It has some . . . velvet draperies in it."

After a moment he said very quietly, "You'd better show me which room it is. You won't have to come any farther than the door."

Crossing to the desk, he opened its drawer and took out a powerful-looking flashlight. In silence we left his room and climbed to the second floor. Up here, with no competition except the flashlight's beam, the glow of the little Scots boy's comet came startlingly bright through the narrow windows. I stopped beside the fourth door. "In there."

Just as before, the door was unlocked. I slumped against the lintel, watching as the flashlight's beam bathed the chest, the scattered armor, the casque now in the far corner of the room, and then the chest again.

Bending, he lifted the lid. For perhaps thirty seconds he gazed at whatever was inside. Then he quietly closed the lid. Turning, he said, "You'd better not look."

I gave an involuntary little cry. He said swiftly, "It's not too bad. It's just that cyanide . . . does things to the face. And it was cyanide. I can still smell it."

I covered my face with my hands. No Enrique for Juanita. No shiny petrol pump. No bright-eyed little son to show off to the tourists.

Cyanide. Who'd forced her to swallow it? No, no. It wouldn't have been done that way. Last night someone had held out a cup or glass to her and said, "Drink this, my girl. It will make you feel better."

Whose face, arranged in a sympathetic smile, had been the last face she saw on earth? Julia Ascoli's? Max Hind's? Nurse Walmsey's? Kurt's? Paul Duvall's? Or the face of the man who stood beside me now, saying, "Don't you think it's time we compared notes?"

22

I LOWERED MY hands. He'd turned off the flashlight. In the glow that came through the narrow windows, his face had an eerie look, the eye sockets dark between brows and high cheekbones, the nose tip casting a spot of shadow on the upper lip.

I echoed dully, "Notes?" The boys must never know. Tommy, especially, must never know that Juanita lay up here among moldering draperies. My heart twisted with a memory of how, down at the villa, Juanita sometimes took time out from her work to hoist him onto her back and gallop with him around the walled rear garden. Although he was a little old for that game, he'd loved it. Arms clasped around her neck, he'd throw back his head and crow with laughter . . .

"Yes, notes. You may be able to tell me things that would help. And there's something I'd better tell you."

"All right," I said, not caring much.

We went down to his room. I sat in the armchair, staring at the floor. Vaguely I was aware that he'd gone into his closet. I heard the snap of suitcase locks, and then, after a moment, the rasping lid of some sort of metal container. He walked over to me, and thrust both hands out to my lowered gaze.

On one palm lay a small shield, bearing words in raised lettering and a number. On the other lay a card bearing the same number, and his photograph and signature. I didn't feel especially surprised, or anything else, for that matter. It had occurred to me last night that he might be some sort of police officer. Not wanting to make excuses for him a second time, I'd rejected the idea.

I looked up at him. "Then you're with Interpol?"

He nodded, and walked back to the closet. Again I heard the rasp of metal. Catching up the desk chair on the way, he moved toward me again. As he sat down, recollection struck me. "Those—those horrible photographs. Were they—?"

"I lied to you a little about those photos," he said gently. "They're not from newspaper files. They represent cases some other Interpol agents are working on. But I am taking them to that Czech psychiatrist."

I'd sensed his lie that night. "And are your press cards fake?"

"No. I'm an accredited correspondent. I was already accredited to that Philadelphia paper when Interpol took me on."

Pain crossed his face. "I never told you this, but the reason I was so eager to get to Paris was that I had an older brother there, ten years older. I grew up thinking Stan was the greatest man in the world. He could do anything—hunt, play basketball, build things. Once he built a studio for himself behind our house singlehanded. And he was a darn good painter. When he was twenty-two and I was twelve, he won a scholarship to study in Paris. He never came back. After a while, he didn't even write more than a couple of times a year."

He paused, and then said more rapidly, "When I finally got to Paris, I found out why. He didn't paint anymore. He was down from a hundred and eighty pounds to a hundred and thirty. He was hooked on heroin, and to finance the habit he was selling dope smuggled in from North Africa. Two months after I got to Paris, he heard Interpol was closing in on him. He shot himself."

I managed to say, "I'm sorry."

"An Interpol agent came to see me. I gave him all the information on Stan that I could, and when he was leaving I said I'd like to work for Interpol. About two weeks later their Paris office called me in for a first interview. They finally took me on, and I've been with them ever since. The publishers of the papers I work for know, of course, but not many other people do."

I said, into the silence, "I can see why you wanted to join them."

"Because of the way Stan died? Yes, that

213

was it." He gave a wry laugh. "But Interpol's like the army. If you want to be a signalman, they're apt to put you to driving a truck. I wanted to help stop the drug traffic. Instead, they've assigned me to about everything else."

"You're after Paul Duvall?" I was trying to care, but my thoughts were up there with Juanita, in that chest surrounded by scattered fake armor. I'd heard that cyanide worked very quickly. I hoped it was true.

"Let's put it this way. I'm up here looking for the same thing Duvall is—a couple of million dollars worth of stolen art. I've searched every place I could, and I suppose he has too. I don't think he's found the pictures, and I know I haven't. That's why I asked Juanita—" He stopped speaking. After a moment he added in a constrained voice, "I thought there was a chance she might bring me some sort of lead."

We were both silent. Then I said, "Does Max Hind know they're stolen?"

"I don't think he even knows they're here. You see, they were stolen years and years ago, during World War Two, from smaller museums all over France and the Netherlands. Most of the art the Nazis looted has been recovered. These paintings weren't. Interpol has been looking for them ever since the war ended. But it wasn't until a few months ago that we had reason to think they were here."

He told me, then, that last spring a middle-aged man, with a long police record, had been killed instantly in a traffic accident in the south of France. His seventy-five-year-old mother had been in the car. She'd lived long enough to tell the police that her son had an associate, a part-time thief, part-time kept man named Paul Duvall. Her son and Duvall had heard several years before that valuable paintings, smuggled across the French border during the chaotic final days of the war, were still hidden in a place called Castle Estillio, now the property of a multimillionaire named Max Hind. As a first step toward making the haul, Paul Duvall had contrived to meet Max Hind's sister. Since then he'd waited for a chance to search Castle Estillio at his leisure. While waiting he'd enjoyed at the Contessa's expense—and, indirectly, Max Hind's—the sort of life to which he'd been accustomed.

"We considered approaching Max Hind directly. But we couldn't be sure he didn't know of the paintings' existence. After all, rich men have harbored stolen art, and even commissioned its theft. If he did know they were here, he'd have stalled for enough time to either destroy the pictures, or transfer them someplace else. We had to get a man in some other way."

I said in a flat voice, "So that's why you approached me that day in San Ysidro. You already knew who I was. You also must have known that Max Hind was recruiting servants and buying station wagons for the trip up here. Probably everyone in San Ysidro was talking about it. So you scraped an acquaintance with me. That way you had an excuse to follow—"

"You're only partly right. I knew Max Hind was getting ready to come up here. And I intended to scrape an acquaintance, as you put it, with some member of his household. But when I first saw you, I didn't know who you were. I just knew you were a pretty girl. And after we'd sat at that sidewalk table for a while, I realized you wouldn't even have had to be pretty for me to like being there."

I said nothing, but in my heart, cold and leaden with the thought of my dead friend, something warm stirred.

He said, "I hope I don't have to tell you how I feel about Juanita. I could say it was

216

in the line of duty, but the truth is that I'll never forgive myself."

"Nor I. I shouldn't have let her go off with Kurt last night. Oh, Len!" I cried. "We've got to find out who killed her!"

He nodded. "And the best way of doing that," he said quietly, "is to find out what terrified her out of her wits last night."

23

I STARED AT him. "You mean, go over there?"

"What else is there to do? If I tackled Max Hind, he'd lie, just as he did in that note. As for his sister, she may be in on it, or she may know nothing about it. Either way, I'd be tipping my hand for little or no information.

"Undoubtedly there's a new guard," he went on, "and he'll be very much on the alert. That's why"—he glanced at his watch—"I'll wait until about one to go over there."

"We." He looked at me questioningly, and I said, "*We'll* go over." I'd let Juanita go over there alone, and she hadn't come back, not alive.

"You think they won't kill a girl? They already have."

"Juanita's mother and sister are poor peasants. Illiterate, too, she told me. They'll accept whatever they're eventually told, and go into mourning for the rest of their lives. But I wrote to my grandparents that I was coming up here. And I've told the Contessa what my grandfather is like. If I disappear —well, he'd come over and tackle our ambassador, he'd go to Interpol, he'd go to the United Nations. If he had to, he'd take this place apart, stone by stone." I paused. "I should imagine they'd think twice about killing an Interpol agent, too."

"They might," he said wryly, "if they gave me a chance to identify myself."

He looked at me for a long, thoughtful moment and then said, "All right. Maybe the two of us would have a better chance." He looked at my brown loafers. "Have you got tennis sneakers?"

"Yes. Shall I put them on now?"

"If you like."

Aware that every nerve in my body had become taut, I slipped down the corridor. In my room, sitting on the edge of the bed, I changed to tennis shoes. As I stood up, my eye fell upon Josiah Ward's book, still resting on the nightstand. Josiah, running his hands over the bricks of that kitchen fireplace . . .

I picked up the book and tiptoed across the bath to the next room. By the night lamp's dim glow, I could see the small figures in the narrow beds. They slept quietly, Steven on his stomach—a sign of stubbornness, my grandmother used to say—and Tommy on his side, one hand loosely curled on the pillow.

Second thoughts struck me. I was the only person in the world they had to love. Was it fair to them to take risks? Without me, anything might happen to them.

But it might anyway. The Contessa had assured me the boys were safe. They weren't. If this place held a human being monstrous enough to kill Juanita, none of us were safe.

I longed to draw Steven's blanket higher over his thin shoulder, and perhaps just touch his little brother's taffy-colored hair. I didn't. They might have awakened.

With the book in my hand, I went back to Len's room. I said, as soon as he'd closed the door, "There's supposed to have been a tunnel, running from beneath the kitchen to the western foot of the mesa."

He said, with a faint smile, "Yes. And

you sneaked a look at an engraving of it one day in this room. Did you know what it was?"

"Not then. Later I realized what it must be. You see, I'd already run across a mention of it." I leafed through the pages until I'd found the right one, and then handed the book to him. "A Bostonian wrote this, back in the eighteen-eighties."

He read for perhaps a minute and then laid the book on his desk. "I felt all over that damn fireplace too."

"And with no better luck than the man who wrote that book?"

"Not in the fireplace. But I found the tunnel entrance. Last night. Or rather, early this morning."

Staring at him, I sank into the armchair. "You mean it really exists?"

"Oh, yes." He sat down in the straight chair opposite me. "Do you know anything about the recent history of this place—the last thirty years, say?"

"Only what I read in a guidebook downstairs. It was written when the man who owned it had opened it to the public. You know, one of those Stately Homes deals. The book said something about the castle having passed through various private hands during this century and the last."

He nodded. "And one pair of those private hands belonged to a rich Nazi sympathizer. He bought it in nineteen forty-two. It must have been some time after that that the paintings were brought here. He died of a stroke in nineteen forty-eight, and his widow, who apparently had never been told that the paintings were here, sold the castle to a Madrid banker.

"The point is," he said, "that part of the kitchen equipment dates from the time the Nazi sympathizer owned this place. At one end of the kitchen, the medieval fireplace is intact. At the other end, Max Hind has installed infrared ovens and mammoth freezers. In between, against the south wall, there's equipment that was the latest thing in the nineteen-forties. Stainless steel wall ovens, for instance—electric ones, but not infrared—set in a steel panel about fifteen feet wide. That equipment obviously isn't used now. I guess Max Hind left it there in case the infrared equipment breaks down."

"And the electric ones have something to do with—"

"I'm getting to that. I'd read about that legendary tunnel, of course, before I got my first look at the kitchen. I figured that if all else failed, I'd try to find the tunnel entrance. But I was sure that the efficient Nazis, if they had stashed loot down there, wouldn't be content with some creaky camouflage device dating from the Crusades, even if they found it still workable, which they probably didn't. No, they would build something new."

"And you found it?"

He nodded. "Around four I decided that Juanita wasn't going to report back, and so I might as well look at those ovens. I took my burglar's kit with me."

"Your what?"

He smiled. "You heard me. Cops have to be good at all the criminal's tricks, or they'd seldom come out ahead. That's why when a cop turns bad he usually makes a damn good safecracker, or loft burglar, or what not. Anyway, I measured the interiors of those three wall ovens. The middle one was a fraction of an inch shallower than the other two. I jimmied out the false back, and there was the button. All I had to do was press. I'd have sworn, by looking at it, that that steel panel didn't have a seam in it. But a section about three feet wide turned on an axis, so that half of it stuck out into the kitchen."

"You—went down there?"

"At four-thirty in the morning? Of course not. Some of the kitchen staff come on duty at five. I shone the flashlight down some nice, clean cement steps that lead to the tunnel. It isn't the way it was described in that old book, so low that men had to bend double. It must be six feet high now, and the granite walls have been finished off with cement.

"After that I pushed the button again. The panel swung closed. I replaced the false rear wall in the oven, and came back here."

No wonder he'd been so sure that no car had driven out of the courtyard, bearing Juanita back to her mother and sister.

He'd been watching me. "I know," he said quietly. "You think a few paintings, even if they are Old Masters, aren't nearly as important as Juanita's life. Or her death, rather. And you are right." He glanced at his watch. "Now I want you to tell me everything she said when she came to your room last night. Don't skip anything."

I frowned. "The trouble is, she skipped things."

"I know. You told me she was pretty incoherent. But tell me what she said."

"Well, she said Carlos—that was the

guard—let her go by. She searched the third floor rooms, and didn't find anything. Then she tried the tower door." Again I frowned. "I think she said, 'It was locked, and I couldn't get in.' " I paused.

"And then?"

"That's where she skipped something. She said, 'And then I could get in, and there was a machine like in office cinemas, and I heard—' She began to cry then, and to say it was terrible, terrible. She made a bolt for the door, and I tried to stop her, and just then Kurt knocked. She went off with him, and that's all."

"Let's take it step by step. She didn't say Carlos had given her keys, and so she was able to unlock the tower door?"

"No. And I think if that had been the case, she'd just have said, 'I unlocked the door.' I think that the way she got in seemed to her too long and too unimportant to tell, compared to what had terrified her in that tower."

He nodded. "And then, when she got to the point of her story, she was too frightened to do anything but cry. Now what's this about a machine like in office cinemas?"

"I don't know. It couldn't have been a

typewriter. She knew that word. I have a typewriter, and so does Steven."

"Besides, you don't 'hear' frightening things from a typewriter, or an adding machine. Seems to me it must have been a tape recorder, or something like that."

"I suppose so."

After a moment he said, "Dinah, you've been afraid here, even before this, haven't you?"

I thought of the things that had filled me with chill unease during my first two days here, when I'd had no idea that my childlike friend would soon lie up there in that stone-floored room. The sentry boxes flanking the road. The unavailability of telephones, radio, TV. That walled-off and guarded eastern side of the quadrangle.

I said slowly, "Yes, I was afraid, even before we reached this place. I looked back at all those trucks and station wagons, and somehow—I was afraid."

"How is it you never talked to me about it?"

"Well, at first I was mad at you, and I didn't trust you. Then for a while everything became so different, so sort of—magical. There was our castle—the one on the mesa, I mean—and you having dinner with us, and taking us up to see the comet each night, and oh, I didn't want to—"

I broke off, appalled at how completely I'd given myself away.

He reached over, smiling, and took my hand. "Aw, Dinah honey, don't look like that."

I let my hand remain in his, but my voice was stiff. "Like what?"

"As if you'd just handed a top-secret file to the Red Chinese. I mean, it's all *right*. I've been way ahead of you all the time. That day in San Ysidro I said to myself, 'I think I'm going to fall in love with this girl.'"

"And?" I tried to keep my voice casual.

"What do you mean, and? I did, that's all. Couldn't you tell that? Now come here."

Standing, he drew me to my feet and into his arms. His kiss seemed to send a kind of sweet shock all through me. Clinging to him, I thought, "Yes, I was right too, that day in San Ysidro."

After a moment he asked, "What is your opinion of marriage?"

Leaning back in the circle of his arms, I asked, in a not quite steady voice, "Speaking generally, or specifically?"

"Very specifically. Marriage for you and me."

"Len, isn't this sort of—?"

He smiled. "Sudden? Well, we could have a long engagement, maybe a month. You could even break off with me a couple times. Aw, Dinah, I do love you so when you act sort of—prim."

We kissed again, and then stood silently in each other's embrace for several moments. At last, raising my head from his shoulder, I said reluctantly, "Len?"

"Yes?"

"Isn't it—time?"

He took one arm free to look at his watch. "About." His voice too was reluctant. "Won't you wait here for me?"

"No. If you didn't come back in an hour, say, I'd go over there alone to look for you, and that might not be so good, might it?"

He said after a moment, "No, it wouldn't. I'll get some things together, and we'll go."

He disappeared into the closet, emerging a few minutes later with a blue canvas satchel, somewhat larger than an airline flight bag.

"What's in it?" He'd been in the closet long enough for my nerves to grow taut, and it showed in my voice.

He looked at me and then said in a casual

tone, "Oh, just some stuff we may need, but probably won't."

Setting the bag on the desk, he went back into the closet. When he came out he was wearing a tan windbreaker. No need to ask why he'd added that garment to his already adequate gray sweater and slacks. I could see the bulge of a shoulder holster under his left arm.

"Always keep behind me, unless I say otherwise. And no talking, of course." He smiled at me. "All set?"

Taking a deep breath, I nodded.

24

WE WENT DOWN the stairwell through the bluish neon glow. Except for the occasional faint sibilance of my tennis sneakers or his crepe-soled shoes, the night seemed utterly silent. After turning into the corridor, we passed the closed doors of the library, the drawing room, the dining room—

He froze. So did I. From up ahead came sounds. The slap of a playing card on a table, and a man's low chuckle, and another man's surly exclamation.

Two guards. Not one man, nodding at this hour, but two men, both wide awake.

Len moved to the door at his left. The knob turned under his hand, and the door swung silently back. At his signal, I followed him into the darkness. Enough light came from the corridor's wrought-iron chandeliers to show me the gleam of a long table's raised edge. We were in the billiard room.

His arm went around me, and his lips whispered directly into my ear. "Bad luck. I'd hoped one karate chop could do it. But we can manage, if you do exactly what I say."

I nodded, hoping that my arm didn't tremble under his hand.

We slipped out of the room and perhaps another thirty feet down the corridor. I saw Len reach inside his jacket. Then he said softly in his atrocious Spanish, "Raise your hands above your heads."

Standing behind him and a little to one side, I had a clear view of the two men at the card-strewn table. They jerked their heads around. Then two pairs of hands shot into the air. The elder of the two men had a gun belt buckled around him, and they both had been provided with visored caps. But under those official-looking visors were the weathered, almost gentle faces of men used to tending vines or raising sheep.

Len said in a barely audible voice, "Dinah." I moved to his side. "You'll have to hold the gun on these men for a few minutes."

I blurted before I thought, "I've never even touched a gun."

He said in Spanish, "You've never touched a gun before? That's good. These men will be very careful to do as I say. They'll know how nervous you'll be." He handed me the gun. "Now put your finger on the trigger, but try not to press it unless I tell you to."

He moved toward the table then, but the cardplayers weren't watching him. Those two pairs of dark eyes were fixed prayerfully on the gun in my not quite steady hand.

Len took the older man's gun and put it in the blue bag. Then, kneeling, he placed the bag on the floor and took from it some objects that jangled faintly. "Put your wrists together," he said to the man on the left-hand side of the table. I realized then that he held handcuffs. They were slim, scarcely thicker than a woman's bracelet. Somehow I'd had the notion that handcuffs were quite massive. He handcuffed one man, then moved to the other. Still those two pairs of frightened eyes stared at the gun muzzle. It was all I could do not to say, "Don't worry. I'm not that nervous."

He snapped the second pair of handcuffs. "Now both of you. Walk very slowly over to the elevator and lie down on the floor beside it, face down. Don't move afterwards, and don't make noise of any sort."

When they'd obeyed—first falling awkwardly to their knees, and then stretching out with their cuffed hands extended beyond their heads—Len picked up the bag and moved swiftly to the shadowy area beside the elevator. As he took what looked like strips of black silk from the bag, and gagged each man in turn, I lowered the gun, with relief, until its muzzle pointed at the floor. Len whipped a length of thin cord from the bag then. Watching him truss the first man, I had a sudden memory of a North Dakota rodeo my grandfather took me to when I was eight. The thin and leathery cowboy who'd won the calf-roping contest had moved as swiftly as Len moved now, but perhaps no more so.

When the second man was trussed, Len walked back to me. Silently he took the gun from my hand and restored it to his shoulder holster. Then he signaled for me to follow him up the stairs. On the landing, I threw a swift look down that luxuriously carpeted corridor with its dark wood paneling, and its crystal chandeliers now dimmed for the night. Then I followed up the second flight of stairs.

Here, stretching away to the right, past the storerooms Juanita had searched about twenty-four hours before, a long strip of rush carpeting lay on the stone floor. But otherwise, bathed in bluish neon glow, it looked exactly like the corridor on the floor above my room.

Directly ahead of us, though, was something radically different. In the lower part of the northeastern round tower, recessed into its rounded surface, were a pair of heavy-looking doors of dark wood, each about six feet wide and ten feet high. I thought, "Why?" Why had anyone needed such a wide doorway?

As I stared at those doors, they seemed to loom taller. But that, I knew, was my fear, my fear of whatever it was beyond those doors that had sent Juanita fleeing to her room to pack her pitiful little suitcase—

Setting down the bag in front of the door, Len knelt on one knee. He took from the bag an instrument that looked like nothing but a thin length of wire, with one end set into a wooden handle. A picklock. I'd never seen one, but I'd heard of them. He inserted the wire into the lock.

Seconds dragged past, perhaps two hundred of them. Once he muttered something under his breath. After a while I saw that his forehead glistened, and I became aware that my own forehead and palms were coldly damp. Through the drumming of my own blood, I strained my hearing for the slightest sound, but, except for the faint scratch of the wire, this whole vast place seemed wrapped in a dead silence.

Then, in that silence, I heard a tiny click. Len sighed, dropped the picklock into the bag, and, carrying the bag with him, stood up. He opened one of the doors, and I followed him inside. Almost without sound, he closed the door behind us.

No narrow stairs spiraling upward. Just a big, hollowed-out, round room. On a broad, flat-topped desk, an ordinary green-shaded student lamp cast a pool of light. Beside the lamp stood a tape recorder. There were spools of tape on the desk, and scattered papers bearing figures and mathematical symbols in a fine hand. To the left, against the curving wall of rough stone, was a table holding a compact shortwave set. The carpet was of ordinary brown pile.

I looked up—and caught my breath. Now I knew why those doors had needed to be so high and wide. Up there, at about the height where, in the northwest round tower, un-railed steps had led up to the trapdoor, was a telescope. Not the sort into which, on boardwalks all over the world, you can slip a coin for the privilege of gazing at ships in the harbor or islands in the bay. I couldn't be sure, but this telescope probably compared in size to those in smaller observatories. It poked its muzzle through a slit in the tower's domed roof. At its other end was an attached viewing seat. Below it, running down to the floor, was the steel column on which the whole apparatus was raised and lowered.

No wonder he'd installed that wide elevator. He'd needed it, not just to carry his crippled body, but to bring the unassembled pieces of this apparatus up here.

For perhaps several minutes, aware that Len's gaze was directed upward too, I stared at the telescope.

"I think it's moving." Even though he spoke in scarcely more than a whisper, his voice echoed in this lofty-roofed room. "I've been watching its shadow on the wall over there, and I'm sure that it's moved, if only a tiny fraction of an inch. The telescope's locked in on something, taking photographs."

Locked in on something.

My mind went blank.

After a moment I thought, "The comet." Of course. Since astronomy was one of his many scientific interests, of course he'd be following the comet. Why had my mind gone blank like that, as if confronted with something unutterable, apocalyptic?

I looked at Len. "Juanita," I whispered.

He nodded. We turned to look at the desk. There it was, of course, the machine-like-you-see-in-office-cinemas.

We walked over to the tape recorder. "Nothing on it now," Len said. He looked over the spools, selected one, and held it out to me. It bore a sticker with the date, September 22, written in the same fine hand as the mathematical calculations covering the scattered papers on the desk. I nodded. The twenty-second was yesterday's—no, day before yesterday's—date. That spool might well have been on the machine when Juanita, awed and yet irresistibly curious, had turned the switch.

Len threaded the spool onto the spindle, attached the tape's end to the other spindle, pressed the switch. For a few seconds, nothing. Then: "I'm right, I'm right, I'm *right!*" Max Hind's exultant voice was so loud that Len leaped to turn the volume down.

"She's back again," that triumphant voice went on, "my five-eyed, ten-tailed serpent —shorn of three of her tails these last two millenniums and a half, but still ready to raise hell. It was a couple of flying rocks that threw her at us, just as I'm sure it was last time. And now, once again, she'll be a pillar of smoke by day, and of fire by night. Seas will part, and cities crumble, and there'll be weeping and lamentation everywhere."

For a moment the tape unwound silently. Then the recorded voice said in a quite different voice, "Position at twenty-two hours, Greenwich mean time: right ascension, one hour, six minutes, thirty-two seconds; declination, plus thirty-five degrees, nineteen minutes, eight seconds. Broadcasts monitored from London, Paris, Washington, Sydney, Moscow, Tel Aviv. All still hewing to the anti-alarmist line, but in the last twenty-four hours a few notes of warning have crept in—"

I turned to Len. "He's crazy, isn't he?" I whispered through the calm voice issuing from the tape recorder. "He is, isn't he?" My voice rose high. "And if he isn't crazy, what does it mean?"

"It means that many journalists, if they're still able to, are going to eat a lot of crow." The voice came from behind me. "No, don't reach for your gun, Mr. Carstairs. Kurt and Ernesto have guns, as you can see, and Miss Haversham is right in the line of fire."

25

FLANKED BY HIS two burly drivers, he sat in his wheelchair a few feet inside the doorway. I thought, with numb detachment, "He looks so much younger." The tired bitterness had gone from his face. His lips smiled. His eyes behind their horn-rimmed glasses were bright.

"Ernesto, turn that machine off. That's right. Now relieve Mr. Carstairs of his gun."

Len stood motionless as the man at Max Hind's left walked to him, reached inside his jacket to take the holstered gun, and returned with it to his place beside the wheel-chair.

"Now, Mr. Carstairs, why don't you bring those two chairs out from the wall so that you and Miss Haversham can be comfortable?"

Not speaking, Len walked over to the shortwave set, seized two leather-bottomed straight chairs that stood beside it, and brought them to the center of the room.

"Sit down, please, both of you." He looked up at Kurt. The German, without being told to do so, moved the wheel-chair close to the desk. Reaching out, Max Hind placed his finger on a button near the desk's edge. "My men will leave us now, but they'll be standing just outside the door with guns drawn, waiting for me to press this alarm. All right, Kurt, Ernesto."

The two men left, with Ernesto closing the door almost silently behind them. "Now, Miss Haversham, you asked the meaning of the tape I made. Let me assure you, first of all, that it does not mean the end of the world. This planet has survived vast convulsions, which in my much-ridiculed opinion have also been quite sudden. Upthrustings of mountains, submergence of islands and continents, reversals of its magnetic poles, and at least two previous visits from that hell-raiser up there." He pointed toward the domed roof. "And the earth is still here. So, I repeat, there is little reason to think that the next seventy-two hours or so will bring what ignorant people in all times have feared, the end of the world."

I said in a thin, flat voice that sounded strange even to my own ears, "Juanita thought it meant the end of the world." ("If you have any family, go to them!")

"Yes, unfortunate, that. She was over here, if I'm not mistaken, on some sort of spying mission for you, Mr. Carstairs."

His eyes, cold now, stared for a moment at the man who sat beside me, one gray-flanneled leg crossed over the other with a nonchalance he couldn't possibly have been feeling. Then Max Hind resumed, "I'd become quite excited while I made that tape. As you may know, I suffer from high blood pressure. Suddenly my vision began to blur, and my head to throb. I switched off the tape and rang for my nurse, Miss Walmsey.

"The girl must have heard the sound of the ascending elevator and dodged into one of the empty storerooms on this floor. I imagine she watched as Miss Walmsey came in here, and then wheeled me out to the elevator. I was in pain. Miss Walmsey was much concerned about me. Neither of us thought to lock the door. But it wasn't until I came back here, calmed by the hypodermic she'd given me, that I knew someone had been at the tape recorder. The unused portion of that tape was still unwinding. I had Miss Walmsey bring that fool of a guard to me. Within five minutes, he'd told me all he knew."

Len said, "And then you sent Kurt over to bring her to you." How did he manage, I asked myself numbly, to keep his voice so casual?

"Yes. I told him my sister had suffered an accident, and needed Juanita. That wasn't true. You may or may not be pleased to hear that my sister is in excellent health. After he'd brought Juanita to me here—and that involved something of a struggle, because she seemed quite out of her mind with terror of this room—I asked him what he had overheard of her conversation with you, Miss Haversham. He said the girl was so hysterical he hadn't been able to understand her, and that apparently you hadn't either."

I asked, "Did you order Kurt to kill her?" Even now, with my mind numbed protectively against things I didn't understand or want to understand, I felt a stir of bitterness against Juanita's murderer.

"Then you know she's dead?" He didn't sound alarmed, just interested.

"Yes. We found her body in the storeroom above my bedroom. Did Kurt kill her?"

"No. The rich, Miss Haversham, can hire almost anything done for them, and I am very rich. But I would not hire anyone to kill a defenseless girl, no matter how necessary the act. And it was necessary. Left alive, she would have spread premature panic inside this palace—something I've taken all sorts of precautions against. She might even have escaped to spread tales about the countryside, which I've been equally determined shall not happen.

"As for the cyanide, I myself gave it to her, in a glass of wine. I brought a small supply with me, to be administered to myself, my sister, and a few others, in case things became too bad."

I stared at him, thinking, "A monster with integrity." Then his last phrase echoed in my memory, and my mind went blank again.

Len said, "But Kurt must have carried her body to that storeroom."

"No. I thought it best not to let him know the girl was dead. He'd been interested in her. I summoned Miss Walmsey, and told her the girl must have suffered a heart seizure. I'm sure she didn't believe that. But —and I hope you won't think me immodest—Miss Walmsey is devoted to me. Too, she must have known that whatever I'd done had been, in my judgment, necessary. I asked her to . . . place the girl somewhere until I could make other arrangements. In the hours since then I have been too busy to do so, too busy, in fact, to even inquire of Miss Walmsey what . . . temporary arrangements she made."

I had a chilled vision of that tall woman, probably in a bathrobe at that hour, carrying Juanita in her arms. Past the drawing room, up two flights of stone stairs to that corridor lit by the comet's glow, and then into that storeroom with its big chest and scattered armor. Len was probably over in the kitchen then, inspecting the wall ovens. The boys were asleep. If her foot hadn't touched that casque and set it rolling, Juanita's body almost surely would have remained undiscovered up there until the "other arrangements" were made.

Max Hind said, "I told her I'd rather not know immediately where she took the girl. I only specified that she not leave her on this

242

side of the quadrangle. I can see," he went on thoughtfully, "why she chose that place. Far too many people move through the kitchen area and the floors above it each day. The western side houses more than a dozen servants, as well as the garage. On the northern side, though, only you two and the children are in residence. Perhaps, too, she recalled some . . . suitable receptacle in that room. When I bought this place, I sent her from England to make a detailed inspection of it, with an eye to whatever changes would be necessary to meet my medical needs. Miss Walmsey is very thorough. I'm sure she looked into every room."

He turned his gaze to Len. "You found the room unlocked?"

"Yes."

"Well, that was not Miss Walmsey's fault. There were no keys to the third floor storerooms among the keys the former owner turned over to me. Perhaps they'd disappeared even before his ownership. Since those rooms contain nothing of real value, I haven't bothered to have keys made."

I said in that same flat voice, "And the guard, Carlos. What did you do with him?"

"I didn't kill him, Miss Haversham, if that's what you're wondering. There was no reason to. He knew nothing of what was on that tape. Besides, he is an able-bodied man, and as such may be useful. For punishment, I gave orders that he is no longer privileged to draw a daily wine ration from the supplies set aside for the servants. I have given him, as you will see"—he smiled faintly—"other responsibilities. I am sure that enforced sobriety, plus the tongue-lashing I gave him, will insure that he'll discharge those duties well."

He looked at Len. "Now, Mr. Carstairs, in a moment I shall be happy to answer any of your questions. But first," he said, his voice growing cold, "I think you owe me some explanations."

Len said nothing. Max Hind went on, "When you first appeared here, I really believed it was because of some romantic attachment to my nephews' governess. What's more, I accepted your story about your arm wound. As the scientific establishment and its journalistic hangers-on are always quick to point out, I am sometimes a gullible man. Later it occurred to me that you might be snooping in pursuit of what your publishers would call 'a Max Hind exclusive.'

"But," he said, his gaze hard, "no newspaperman I ever heard of equips himself with handcuffs, gags, and nylon rope. Incidentally, didn't it occur to you that I might not only double the guard, but arrange for a foot patrolman too? I think he must have found those handcuffed men, and awakened me, about the time you succeeded in picking the lock of this door. That is how you got in, isn't it?"

"Yes."

"I imagine the picklock is in that blue bag near your chair. Well, in due time, Kurt will take charge of the bag for you. Now tell me why you broke into this room, Mr. Carstairs. And why did you send that girl over here where she had no business to be?"

"I've been looking for some paintings, Mr. Hind. They were stolen about thirty years ago from museums in France and the Netherlands. You see, I am a journalist, but I'm also an Interpol agent."

"Are you, now?" He sounded only mildly interested. "Well, I know nothing of any paintings. If they were placed here, it must have been during some former ownership. The fine arts have never interested me. If I'd known the location of the pictures, and known you wanted them, you could have had them, freely."

He'd spoken indifferently, and in the past-perfect tense, as if a dozen Old Masters no longer mattered. Could it be that they didn't? Were all the agonized El Grecos in the world, and serene Raphaels, and sensuous Titians, potentially just scraps of fuel for—

"All right, Mr. Carstairs." He leaned back in his wheelchair. His wide shoulders looked relaxed. His eyes were confident, even happy. Only his crooked, big-knuckled forefinger, touching the alarm button, held tension. "Fire your questions."

26

AFTER A MOMENT Len said slowly, "I'm not Willy Ley, or Robert Sullivan, or any other science writer—"

"How I wish you were, Mr. Carstairs! How I'd love to have about half a dozen of those fellows here!"

"—and so I guess the only question I have is, what's going to happen?"

"That's a question nobody can answer, not with any degree of exactitude. However, you might be interested to know that in the event of any serious natural disturbances, this structure is about as safe as any place you could find. We are fifty miles from the sea. This mesa is solid granite, and there is no known geological fault in the whole area. Not that I bought this place because of those factors. I had no idea four years ago that a youngster in Scotland was going to spot that hazy patch in the sky. I investigated this area's record of seismic activity merely because such matters interest me, not because I had any thought that they would become personally important to me."

"When did you decide that they were personally important?"

"You see, Mr. Carstairs, you do have questions. It was many, many weeks ago, when I read—and then observed for myself—that the supposedly new comet had five nuclei. That fact alone was not conclusive. It was the additional fact of its being multitailed which made me sure that this was indeed the ten-tailed, five-eyed serpent, come back to us again."

"The comet has only seven tails." My voice still had that thin, colorless quality.

"Only six now, Miss Haversham. It lost a tail about fifteen hours ago. Comets often do. As you may know, those tails are made up of meteoric particles, thrown out by the nucleus or nuclei, and forced back from the head by the pressure of the sun's radiation. Those tails represent a permanent energy loss which occurs whenever a comet's orbit brings it near some source of excitation such as our sun. If the loss is too great, a tail will disappear entirely. Although still unusually heavy, this particular comet must have lost a great deal of mass and energy since it visited us some twenty-five hundred years ago."

"You seem so sure that it did." Len's voice, like mine, now had a peculiar flatness.

"Yes! Long ago, quite independently of Velikovsky, I decided that a giant comet had approached earth at least twice, leaving the record of its visits in many forms. There is the physical record of the first visit in the earth itself. For instance, in Siberia, frozen in the ice, are prehistoric flora and fauna of the arctic and temperate zones—woolly mammoths and wolves and giant turtles— all in a vast tangle, and many with still-undigested food in their stomachs, as if some sudden convulsion of the earth and sea had swept them together. On a later visit, the comet left its record in the minds of men. The chapter of Exodus in the Old Testament, with its parting seas, its trembling earth shrouded in dust, is, I firmly believe, an eye-witness account of that visit. So are the so-called legends and myths of many peoples—the Polynesians, various African tribes, and the pre-Columbian inhabitants of North and South America."

He broke off, and then said, "But perhaps you haven't heard of Velikovsky."

I shook my head. Len said, "Vaguely."

"He too has been called an ignoramus and a crackpot. And much as I hate to agree in any particular with the scientific establishment, I too feel he is mistaken in the belief that the comet of twenty-five hundred years ago went into an orbit around the sun, and now appears in our morning and evening skies as the planet Venus. No, my belief is that after its last visit, the Five-eyed Serpent swung far out on its orbit, leaving the men of earth free to found and overthrow their ancient empires, venture across oceans, fight their Crusades and their revolutions and their two World Wars, and take their first steps into space. But now her path has brought her back to us."

For perhaps a minute there was silence, there in the big circular room under the shadowy dome. Was he mad? Surely he was—or at least grossly in error. Surely that lovely thing streaming across the sky had already started moving away into lonely space, just as those newspapers Len had read had said it would. It couldn't be that it had moved closer, and would move closer still, changing from an object of awed delight into a source of terror and desolation.

Len said, "Did Velikovsky invent the name Five-eyed Serpent?"

"He did not! I did—or rather, I discovered it. Since neither of you have been interested in such matters, it is extremely unlikely that you've heard of an article I published in nineteen sixty-five, in a scientific journal I founded. In it I described interpretations I'd made, aided by a young archaeologist, of hieroglyphics I'd discovered in Peru and Yucatán. As I interpreted them, there were references to a ten-tailed, five-eyed serpent which in the distant past had descended from the sky to wreak havoc of the sort described in Exodus—dust storms, earthquakes, and displacement of rivers and seas. All but a few scientists ignored my article, of course, and those few ridiculed it. One Australian archaeologist inquired sarcastically why I hadn't decided that the Medusa, with its head of writhing snakes, represented a racial memory of my rampaging comet."

Len said, "On that tape you mentioned something about flying rocks—"

"As I'm sure you know, Mr. Carstairs, there are an estimated fifty thousand asteroids—little worlds less than one mile to about five miles wide—traveling in a broad orbital belt between Jupiter and Mars. Modern astronomers, with their attention focused on stars ten billion light years away, pay as little attention to asteroids as they do to comets. Science hasn't even bothered to plot the orbits of the overwhelming majority of asteroids.

"Perhaps my natural perversity led me to pay attention to those flying rocks that the so-called real scientists have neglected. Anyway, I've studied them closely. And although I'm only an amateur, I'm an amateur with a computer—at my place in England. With its aid I've plotted the orbits of thousands of those little worlds. Long ago it occurred to me that if a comet had made a close approach to earth at the time of Exodus, it could have been deflected toward us by the magnetic field of one of the larger asteroids, or by the combined magnetic influence of two or three small ones, if they were lined up just right."

He stopped speaking. After a moment Len asked, "And that did happen, this time?"

"Yes. But when it happened, who except amateurs were bothering to track the comet closely? And they had no equipment with which to check the tiny swerve in the comet's path then. That swerve was scarcely measurable. But after an object has traveled a hundred million miles or so, any deviation from its earlier path becomes very great indeed. I can't say at just what point my scientific betters perceived the change. I do know that several days ago they began to admit publicly that McGrath's comet had left its previously predicted orbit."

I said, "If you're right, if there is to be . . . trouble, and you foresaw it, why didn't you give out warnings? You could have called press conferences, taken newspaper ads—"

"And been laughed at again?" His voice was bitter. I thought of my father's article, and its description of how one of Max Hind's predictions of some years ago—that Vesuvius would erupt disastrously within a few months—had earned him the ridicule not only of scientists, but of cartoonists and TV comics.

"No," he said, still bitterly, "I decided to

252

bring my sister and my nephews here, to-gether with enough servants to secure their comfort, and, if necessary, their defense."

I asked thinly, "Defense?"

"My dear Miss Haversham, among those supplies I had brought here are food con-centrates sufficient for us all for weeks, even months. But if I am right about the days ahead, refugees will soon descend upon any source of food, like locusts settling upon a field of wheat. That's why I could not risk allowing that girl to spread premature panic in this place. At least a few others might have tried to leave. If even one had succeeded, the countryside for miles around would have known that here was not only high ground, but literally tons of food."

I remembered the seemingly odd fancy that had struck me when, just before we started up onto the mesa, I'd looked back at that line of trucks and station wagons. Max Hind *had* been preparing for a siege.

Len asked in a carefully controlled voice, "And if you're wrong?"

"You mean, if our visitor passes by with-out giving us much more than a good scare? Astronomers are still predicting that, at least officially. Well, in that case, my sister and I and everyone here will have had an interesting change of scene for a short time. I shall dismiss, with thanks and a small bonus, all but my regular staff of servants. I'll return to England. My sister and our nephews and my sister's friend"—his lip curled slightly —"will return to San Ysidro. And no one will be the wiser about the real reason for our coming here."

Len and I would be the wiser. And not just about his elaborate preparations for a disaster that never happened, but also about his giving cyanide to a terrified and innocent girl.

That is, if we were allowed to live.

I felt an odd stilling of all my senses.

Then I heard Len ask, in a voice that seemed to come from far away, "What are the chances that you're right?"

Max Hind shrugged. "Why not estimate them yourself? If you step over to that short-wave set, you'll hear the sort of broadcast the whole world has been hearing for several days now. But don't move in this direction, Mr. Carstairs. Keep in mind that my finger still touches this button."

Getting up from his chair, Len crossed in front of me to the shortwave set. He flipped a switch.

"—no cause for great alarm," a man's

voice said in Spanish. "However, merely as a precaution, inhabitants of all seacoast areas are advised to seek higher ground—"

Len turned the dial. "—deflected from its previous orbit by the combined magnetic influence of two asteroids in the belt between Mars and Jupiter," a voice said in unflappable BBC English. "There is no present reason to believe—repeat, no present reason to believe—that there will be a collision between the comet and the earth. Even if such a collision occurred, the effect would be no more than that of the impact of a large meteor. If the impact point were an inhabited area, there might be loss of life, but the disaster would be localized, affecting at most a few dozen square miles. If a comet struck any of the world's oceans, a tidal wave, of proportions not previously predictable, might result.

"But we emphasize that no such collision is expected. We are asked to prepare ourselves for the possibility of atmospheric and even seismic disturbances as the comet approaches and then passes earth. There may be winds of high velocity, accompanied by sandstorms in the drier regions. Higher tides are almost certain to occur. Along fault lines already under stress, such as those running

255

through California and the islands of Japan, earth tremors may be felt.

"We emphasize that none of these disturbances may take place, and that even if they do, the loss of life will probably be minor. In short, there is no cause for great alarm. However, merely as a precaution, inhabitants of seacoast areas are being advised to seek—"

Again he switched the dial. "—message is being broadcast continuously," a voice said in French, "by all radio and television networks.

"The twelve midnight statement, Greenwich mean time, issued by members of the International Astronomical Association gathered at the Royal Observatory, Edinburgh, reads as follows:

" 'It is now evident that McGrath's comet will pass much closer to earth than was expected. The massive comet was deflected from its previous orbit by the combined magnetic influence of two asteroids in the belt between Mars and Jupiter. There is no present reason to believe—repeat, no present reason to believe—that there will be a collision between the comet and the earth. Even if such a collision—' "

Len moved the dial. A voice spoke in German. I know almost no German, but I did recognize a series of numbers. The words had that singsong quality which many announcers' voices take on when they give a weather report. This, I realized, was almost certainly no report of the weather, but of the comet's last observed position.

Apparently Len could understand German, because he listened until the voice ceased, and then, perhaps thirty seconds later, resumed. I heard Len mutter, "Same thing all over again."

Switching off the set, he turned and looked at Max Hind. "So?"

The gray-haired man smiled. "So."

"It looks as if you may be able to serve several portions of crow."

"Perhaps. Perhaps I'll even be able to force them to eat it. On the other hand, when I tell of the preparations I made, they may try to convince themselves and each other that mine was just a lucky guess, and that my theory about the Five-eyed Serpent is still just another of my crackpot ideas."

After a moment Len asked, "Are Miss Haversham and I excused now?"

"Surely you're not serious, Mr. Carstairs. Do you think that, after all the precautions I've taken to keep order here as long as possible, I'd let you two roam around freely? You are both too enterprising for me to allow that. Because of the knowledge she now has, Miss Haversham would be almost certain to try to communicate with her grandparents, thus—to use a military term—breaking security here. And since your journalistic cover, as I imagine Interpol calls it, is a real one, you'd be almost certain to try to communicate with one of your publishers. I and I alone will talk to the press, if and when I can be sure that the measures I have taken here will not make me a laughingstock again."

"And if we promised to talk to no one?"

"I wouldn't accept your promises. No, Mr. Carstairs, you and Miss Haversham will be under detention, at least for the next few days. I provided ahead of time for some such contingency as this, and so I don't think you'll find yourselves too uncomfortable—unless, of course, you are foolish enough to alarm members of my staff."

I said, "You mention the next few days. Does that mean—"

"Yes, Miss Haversham," he broke in, "the comet's effects, whether severe or mild, are expected to start manifesting themselves at any time. According to previous messages from the gentlemen gathered in Edinburgh, the effects will persist for perhaps three days, and then subside as the comet moves away."

I leaned forward. "Mr. Hind, don't separate me from Steven and Tommy. They're still little boys. Steven won't even be nine until next Thursday. Under any circumstances, they'd be unhappy and frightened to find me gone. And now—"

"I'm sorry, but I don't need you to tell me my duty toward my nephews. They will be well cared for. I will give instructions that they are to be told you've been called back to America for a few days."

"Please. Oh, please! You don't understand them, Mr. Hind, and I do. Their needs are greater than most children's. After their mother's death they were so—so emotionally starved—"

"Miss Haversham! If you want to see my nephews again, you'll cooperate with me now."

I didn't see him press the call button, but he must have, for Kurt and Ernesto came in.

27

IT WAS ERNESTO who marched us, drawn gun at our backs, down the northeast staircase to the second floor, then the first. "Turn left to the first door," he said in Spanish. Then: "Open it."

Len opened it, a door of heavy oak. More steps. At their foot, a similar door.

We must be below ground level now. Detention rooms, beyond that door? Undoubtedly. And in a place like this, detention rooms were called—

My mind recoiled from the word. Surely it wouldn't be like that. Max Hind had installed infrared ovens, and central heating, and air conditioning. Surely, down here, we wouldn't find stone floors, and matted straw for beds, and chains that had been bolted into walls centuries ago.

Ernesto ordered Len to knock. Almost immediately the door opened. The man who stood there, bathed in the bluish neon light that illuminated the short corridor stretching behind him, was the ugliest I'd ever seen. The broken-veined face under the visored cap was bulbous-nosed, heavy-lipped, sloping-chinned. Buckled around his consider-able girth was a holstered gun. He stepped aside, and Len and I, at Ernesto's order, moved down three steps onto a cement floor.

Vaguely I was aware of a side passageway, narrow and unlighted, stretching away to my left. Ahead of us was the wide main corridor. On both sides of it were two steel doors, set with a barred rectangular grill about five feet above the floor. With a hysterical impulse toward laughter, I realized I actually felt re-lieved. Surely, behind such a door, I wouldn't find dripping walls, or a foul-smell-ing straw bed—or rats.

With one of a bunch of keys dangling from a ring attached to his belt, the guard un-locked the first door on the right. Ernesto waved his gun to indicate Len was to go inside. The door clanged shut. With a sim-ilar gesture, he ordered me into the next cell. Again that steel clang.

By the mingled light of neon tubing be-hind me and the glow of the Scots boy's comet coming through the barred, high-up window, I saw that even though the walls, like the floor, were stone, they didn't drip. And there was a real bed, a narrow one with head and foot of white painted metal, spread with a blanket and turned-back sheet.

What's more, over there in the left-hand rear corner, two narrow wooden walls had been erected to form, together with the cell's stone walls, a sort of tall cabinet.

There was a door in the cabinet. I opened it. Yes, I'd been right. Again I felt that wild impulse to laugh. There was also a small stainless-steel washbasin, about the size you find on interurban trains.

I shut the door and, turning, found my jailer staring at me, over the small metal tray affixed to my side of the grilled door. For the first time I became aware of the eyes set—no, imprisoned—in that ugly face. Large and dark and sad, they were the eyes of a romantic, a poet, a lover of fair women.

"Are you Carlos?" He'd given Carlos "other responsibilities," Max Hind had said, and had smiled as he spoke.

The ugly face scowled. *"Silencio!"*

I heard the closing of the oak door that led to the stairs. The guard looked in the direction of the sound, then back at me. He nodded. "Juanita?" he asked, after a moment.

I looked into the sad brown eyes of the forever-imprisoned Carlos. No wonder he drank. "I don't know," I lied.

He moved away. After a moment I heard

the creak of wood. Evidently he'd lowered his bulk into the chair beside the door leading to the stairs.

Turning, I looked at the high-barred window. The narrow shelf of earth that ran along the castle's northern base must be out there. I took off my shoes and stood on the blanketed bed. Yes, by craning my neck I could see a short stretch of that ledge. The light that bathed it, and illuminated the empty space beyond, no longer looked like the flooding radiance of a harvest moon. A sullen, reddish tint had crept in—

"Dinah?"

I got down off the bed and, not bothering to put on my shoes, hurried to the door. I crowded as close to the grill as the little metal shelf would allow. "Yes?"

"Is your cell equipped with what the English refer to as a loo?"

"It certainly is."

"*Silencio!*"

I asked in Spanish, "Why can't we talk? We can't get out, and even if we did, you've got a gun."

Carlos muttered something indistinct, and then lapsed into silence.

"Darling?"

"Yes. Yes, Len."

"If he was going to be so damn humane about it, why couldn't he have put us in the same cell?"

"Oh, Len!" I began to cry.

"Stop it, Dinah. Stop it, sweetheart, or that's the last gallant remark you'll ever hear from me."

Taking a deep breath, I pressed my fingertips hard against my closed eyelids. He asked, *"Parles-tu française?"*

"Oui."

"Of course you do," he went on in French. "I'd forgotten. Well, it will be safer. He must know some English. Dinah, I'll try to get us out of here, somehow."

I didn't answer immediately. So he too didn't think this was just a matter of a few days' detention.

I said, forcing the words from a dry throat, "He means to kill us, doesn't he?"

For almost a minute he didn't answer. Then he said, "Dinah, I don't see how he can afford not to. But cheer up. If he's right about that damned comet, he's going to have his hands too full to bother with us right away. Perhaps, by the time he gets around to us . . ."

"Yes," I said. Despite my best effort, my tone sounded false. "Yes, of course."

"Think you can get some sleep now, or at least some rest? It may be important later on."

Sleep. Steven and Tommy, as I'd last seen them, deep in the calm-breathing sleep of childhood. They'd have how many more hours of sleep? Four? Three? And then they'd awaken to a world from which I'd vanished—

Suddenly I grabbed the metal shelf and hung on. This whole structure of ancient stone had been given, as if by a giant hand, a brief, sharp shake.

28

RELUCTANTLY I AWOKE from blessed sleep into the enduring nightmare. How long had I been asleep this time? Two hours, three? And was it daytime now, or night? Without asking the guard, it was impossible to be sure. Wind-driven dust keened past the barred window like some endlessly unrolling backdrop. Through its sullen reddish light —the sun's? the comet's?—filtered into the cell to mingle with the neon glow from the corridor.

How long had we been down here? Hadn't

there been part of a night, and then a day and a night, and then another day? Anyway, I'd been served six different meals, and the last one, beef ragout, had surely been dinner. Suddenly ravenous after those other meals which I'd barely tasted, I'd sat on the bed's edge and wolfed down the ragout and the small loaf of bread which had accompanied it. I'd returned the bowl to the shelf under the grill, and then fallen asleep—but not, I was sure, for more than a few hours. Carlos must be on duty now, rather than the day-time guard who brought the meals.

He was young, that second guard, scarcely out of his teens, and literally speechless with fright. The barely controlled panic in his face enabled me to picture the hysteria upstairs, and the difficulty Max Hind and the upper servants must be having to maintain any sort of discipline. Whenever I spoke to the young guard he just glared, trying to mask his fear with apparent rage.

But from Carlos—his broken-veined face wearing the drawn look of enforced abstinence—I'd learned that the assembled household had been told by Max Hind that it was the comet which had raised this shroud of dust, and caused the earth, like some fly-tormented beast, to twitch its skin now and then. The disturbances might grow worse, they'd been told. But they were safer here than they might be in almost any other place. And soon, as the comet moved away, the earth would grow quiet, and the air clear.

Len and I had talked at intervals during the last forty—fifty?—or more hours. But not of the comet. No, never of the comet, not even when rainless lightning, followed by rainless thunder, had lit the dust beyond the barred windows. We'd talked of Wisconsin, and of North Dakota, and of whether or not those fishermen along the Seine ever caught anything. We talked of where we'd live after we married. Just as some couple who'd spent all their lives in one place might talk hopefully of working abroad for their first year or two together, Len and I talked of settling down for a while. He'd ask a release from Interpol, and then try to wangle from his publishers some sort of stationary assignment for a year or so, preferably somewhere in the United States. A friend of his, who had an apartment near New York's Lincoln Center, had talked of giving it up.

Once we'd tried to speak of Steven and Tommy. I'd had a vision of them—huddled white-faced in each other's arms against their bewildered aloneness, their terror of the

267

lightning-riven chaos outside—and I'd broken into sobs that even Len's soothing voice couldn't stop. After that we hadn't mentioned the boys.

Getting up from the bed, I moved to the grill. "Len?" I called softly. No answer. He was asleep.

Turning, I went back to the narrow bed and lay on my side, staring at the rough stone wall. Glad as I was that he slept, I longed to have him wake up and call my name as softly as I'd called his.

Instead I heard a knock on that heavy door to the stairs. The legs of Carlos' chair scraped over the stone. A key grated in a lock. Carlos said, "Young gentleman! You can't come in here!"

"I brought something for you, in this basket."

My heart seemed to stop for a moment, and then begin to throb through my whole body. Steven's voice. *Steven's.* How had he known? Had someone deliberately told the boys I was down—No, nobody could be that cruel. Surely, just as Max Hind had promised, they'd been told I'd been "called back to America." Then how—? Steven must have overheard servants' gossip. Some people, far from remembering that little

268

pitchers have big ears, seem to think they have no ears at all.

"If you'll let me in," Steven said in a high, too-bright voice I'd never heard him use before, "you can have these."

The hinges were well oiled. I didn't hear the door swing back. I just heard Steven's small feet descending the three stone steps to the neon-lit corridor.

The door closed. A cork made a sucking sound as it was withdrawn from a bottle. I heard a liquid gurgle. No clink of bottle against glass. Almost as if he stood before me, I could see Carlos tilting the bottle to his lips, letting its contents flow down his drink-famished gullet.

Steven must have gotten the bottle—bottles?—from that liquor cabinet in the drawing room. Surely it was a measure of the confusion on the floors above that he'd been able to make his way up here, unhalted and perhaps even unnoticed.

"Thank you, young gentleman, but you'd better go now."

"If you'll let me stay for a while, I'll bring you two more bottles tomorrow."

A pause. That gurgling sound. My surprised immobility left me, and I swung my feet off the bed.

269

"All right." Then, sternly, as if clinging to a remnant of his custodial authority: "But you can't talk to the prisoners. Nobody talks to the prisoners."

"I don't want to talk to any old prisoners!" The voice was loud, tinged with warning. Halfway to the grilled door, I halted. "I just want to see a dungeon."

"All right." Clink of a bottle against the stone floor. "I'll boost you up."

I pictured Steven, thin little waist grasped by Carlos' big hands, and small fingers clinging to the grill of the door opposite Len's. Was he awake now? Surely he was. But he too must have caught the warning in Steven's voice, because he'd made no sound.

"See?" Carlos said. "Not bad at all in there, is it?"

"Can I see the next one?"

"It's the same as this."

"But I want to see!"

"All right." His tone was impatient, as if he longed to turn back to that bottle.

Silently I retreated to my bed and sat down. Two pairs of footsteps, one heavy, one light, drawing close. They stopped. After a moment Carlos said, "See, it's just the same."

I gripped the edge of the bed with both

hands. If I could just catch a glimpse of him, the back of his head, his thin little neck— But he'd feel my gaze, and he'd have to turn, and I must look hideous now, with my hair uncombed, and no lipstick. For his sake and mine, I mustn't. Besides, there'd been that warning in his high, strained little voice.

"I'm nine." Carlos must have set him down. His voice came from just outside my door. "I was nine yesterday."

Of course you were. Do you think I'd forget when your birthday was?

The footsteps retreated. Scrape of glass against stone. Gurgle of liquid. *"Hola!"* Carlos said, as if in sudden realization. "Shouldn't you be in bed?"

"It doesn't matter. Felicia won't know I got up again." He raised his voice. "Felicia gets us up, and brings trays, and puts us to bed. But after that she goes away. She doesn't give lessons."

Who was Felicia? One of the housemaids, probably. I hoped she liked children.

"Well, anyway, you'd better go now." His voice had thickened.

"If you don't like that kind, I'll bring you another kind tomorrow night."

A long pause. "This kind's fine. All right.

271

You can sit there on the steps for a while."
The wooden chair creaked.

"I can do long division."

"*Verdad?*" From Carlos' tone, I could tell he didn't know what long division was.

"I can divide three numbers into five numbers. I did it just this morning. And I gave my brother a spelling lesson, and he spelled friend right, and niece, and chief. He's always getting i-e words wrong, but this morning he got them right."

A progress report. He was giving me a progress report. I drew a deep breath, and bit my lower lip. The thought of them bent over their study table, trying to carry on the routine I'd designed for them—

"My brother and I, we built a castle out on the mesa, a little one."

"*Verdad?*"

"In San Ysidro we have a merry-go-round that plays music."

He chattered on. After a while Carlos stopped saying, "*Verdad?*" Through the tense young voice I heard, at what seemed almost regular intervals, the sound of liquid pouring through a bottleneck. Steven had been there not more than twenty minutes when, through his feverish chatter about baseball, I heard a second cork being drawn.

For perhaps another ten minutes Steven went on, describing the Telestar broadcast of the World Series he'd seen the previous fall. Then his voice died. For a while after that there was no sound except, at intervals, that gurgling. Finally even that ceased. The bottle dropped without breaking, as if from a hand dangling almost to the floor, and rolled noisily for two or three seconds. More silence, and then a snore.

I sat there, fighting with my urge to tiptoe to that grill and call Steven's name softly. I mustn't. By now I was sure of what he intended to do. It would be best to let him do it his way.

Yes, there was the sound I'd expected, the subdued clink of key against key.

A snore breaking off in the middle. Creak of wood. A muttering. Just as Steven must have, I froze, breath held.

Another long snore. After a minute or two, that subdued clinking again. Aware of sweat on my upper lip, I pictured those small fingers struggling to pull the heavy key ring apart.

A click. A small irrepressible sigh. No jangle of keys now. He must have closed his other hand around them.

I heard no sound of tiptoeing footsteps. But surely he must be moving to a point opposite Len's door. He'd have to toss them through a grill with bars set too close together to admit even my hand more than a few inches above the wrist, let alone Len's. "Don't let him miss!" I prayed. Even a drunken man might be aroused by keys striking a steel bar, and then falling back to the stone floor only five feet or so from his chair. But if they went through, and Len caught them, as he surely would—

Very softly, the door to the stairs opened and then closed.

29

WEAK WITH SURPRISE and disappointment, I huddled there on the bed. Why, after all that, had he left, simply left? It must be that, at the last moment, his courage had failed. No one, I least of all, could blame him for that. He was a child, a very bright one, but still a child, alone in a world where even the lordly adults were terrified.

"Dinah?" It was little more than a whisper.

I moved swiftly and silently to the grill. "Yes, Len?"

The snoring stopped.

Len said nothing more. Neither did I. Rigidly I stood there, until the snoring resumed. Then I moved slowly back to the bed. It creaked faintly as I lay down. Then there was no sound except the dust-laden wind blowing past the barred window, punctuated now and then by a rumble of thunder. Had any of those voices we'd heard over the shortwave nights and nights ago—no only three nights—had any of them mentioned that there might be thunder and lightning as well as dust storms? I couldn't remember. It was electromagnetic discharges, Len had said, which were causing "the racket." Was that what caused all lightning? I had no idea.

I wondered if Steven was back in his room with Tommy now. Perhaps he was lying face down on his bed, sobbing over his failure. Or perhaps he was gathering his courage for another try. In a way, I desperately hoped he was. But in another—well, it wasn't that he'd reap severe punishment. His uncle, as Len had said, wasn't cruel for the fun of it. Max Hind might decide, though, to make sure that Len and I caused no further trouble.

Trouble. What troubles were others suffering while Len and I were shut up down here, cut off from contact with anyone except two ignorant and frightened men? Was the havoc less than those cautious voices on the radio had predicted? Worse? Everything within me tightened up at a vision of waves crashing against the steps of St. Paul's, foaming above the flower beds of Rockefeller Center. For perhaps the twentieth time, I felt thankful that my grandparents lived hundreds of miles from any large body of water.

Suddenly I felt tired, tired. It seemed to me that I had been down here for years. And for what? When Max Hind finally did have that door unlocked, it would mean—No, no. We'd think of some argument, Len and I, some threat, *something*, to keep ourselves alive. But right now, I was too tired even to think about keeping alive.

I closed my eyes.

Perhaps I even dozed, because I had no idea how much later it was that I heard a soft "Dinah!"

Not Len's voice. Steven's.

And not from the corridor, but from—

For perhaps three seconds, frozen, unable to move, let alone turn and look, I just lay there. Then I swung myself upright on the bed's edge, jerked my head around, and clutched my throat to strangle the scream welling up inside it.

He was out there, on that narrow ledge, his small body outlined against that moving curtain of dust, with that sullen glow behind it. As he crouched there, both hands grasping the window bars, his little bottom must be projecting out over—

"Dinah, we've been so scared without you."

Watch what you say. Don't startle him.

"Darling, you've brought the keys, haven't you?" I could see them, dully gleaming, and apparently suspended from twine he'd tied around his neck. "Now don't throw them to me." Above all, he mustn't let go of those bars. "Wait'll I move the bed over. I'll climb up and get the keys. And then somehow we'll help you off that—"

"No."

"*Steven!*"

"I'll give them to Len. You're not much good with keys, Dinah. You'll make a lot of noise, and wake that man up."

Oh, God! Why had he had to remember

I usually had trouble unlocking doors? Should I climb up on the bed and try to—No, no! He might try to dodge away from me and—

"I've got a rope around me, see? I got it from the round tower. I tied the other end to that stick in the middle of a window in the big room. I tied four knots in it."

The drawing room. The partition in the center of one of those casement windows.

"So even if I do fall, I won't get killed."

My stomach turned over. His little body, dangling out there in the windy murk, perhaps banging against the mesa's rocky wall—

"I'll see you on my way back," he whispered.

Frozen, helpless, I watched his left hand shoot out to grasp some protuberance, invisible to me, on the outer wall. He was moving now. His right hand released one bar, slid to another and grasped it, and then another and another. Then the window was empty except for the bars, and the moving dust curtain, and an angry flicker of lightning. I stood rigidly motionless. I think I was trying to will equal stillness on the earth's unquiet crust, trying to will that no tremor shake the rough stone wall as he inched his way along it.

By what agonizing expansion of his intelligence, his just-turned-nine courage, had he moved from that drawing room window out onto the ledge?

For an eternity I stood there. Even though I strained my ears, I could hear nothing but the wind's monotonous voice. He'd fallen. He'd slipped over into those murky depths without a cry, a word—

Small fingers grasped the window's right-hand bar, moved to the next one. His upper arm came into view, his chest. And then he went into that deep, terrifying crouch.

"He's got them, Dinah. You'll come to us? Right away? Just as soon as you get out?"

"Oh, yes." My whisper sounded as if my throat had been sandpapered. I added, because I couldn't help it, "Be careful. Don't hurry."

"I won't. And it seems wider out here to me than it would to you. Now you'll come to us right away?"

"Yes." My voice cracked. "Steven, please go."

I watched the right hand disappear, then the left. I went into the cabinet and was sick. I rinsed out my mouth. Then I moved to the bed and dropped onto it, face down. Through the blood churning in my ears I heard, a few yards away, a key turn in the lock of a steel door.

30

SECONDS LATER MY door opened. Len moved to me and put his hand on my shoulder. "You all right?" he asked softly.

"Yes, but I'd better not . . . try to stand up just yet."

"I know. Why, for a minute I too almost—Anyway, just stay there. I can manage for a while."

His feet in their crepe-soled shoes moved soundlessly away. After perhaps a minute, a raucous snore broke off in the middle. I heard, or thought I heard, the sound of a blow. A fist to the jaw? A karate chop? Fleetingly, I wondered if Carlos believed in an afterlife, where things were evened up for people like him.

A dragging sound. The noisy roll of an empty bottle. I felt strong enough to stand now. I moved out into the corridor. The door to Len's cell stood open. Neon light shone down on the empty chair with one amber bottle standing beside it, and another bottle on its side a few feet away, label side up. It had held brandy.

"Len?"

His voice came from inside the cell. "Couple of minutes."

When he emerged from the cell he was wearing Carlos' blue cotton shirt and trousers, their bagginess held in by a tightly cinched belt. The visored cap shadowed his face. On his left hip, Carlos' gun hung in its holster.

"Bad fit for me, but mine are worse for him." His gaze lingered on my face for a moment. "He'll have a stiff neck for a few days, that's all."

He closed the cell door, locked it. I watched him silently. It would be a waste of time to ask him what he intended to do. I'd find out soon enough.

"Come on." To my surprise he led me, not toward the door onto the stairs, but down the narrower passageway that ran at right angles to the main corridor. The door at its end was locked. After several tries, he found the key that fitted. Swinging the door back, he motioned for me to go ahead.

I stepped onto hard-packed earth. He followed, closing the door, and we were left with utter darkness and the smell of centuries. Damp rock, and soil that hadn't known the sun's warmth since long before Columbus sailed.

"The vaults." Even though no one possibly could have heard us, his voice was hushed. "Maybe they used to keep wine down here. There's nothing now."

I wondered how he knew, and then remembered an expansive Max Hind giving him the freedom of the premises. Obviously Len had made the most of that freedom, even investigating the forbidden eastern quadrangle at its below-ground level.

"Power plant up ahead. Just hook your fingers over my belt and hang on. And don't talk when we go through the next door. There should be a man on duty."

After we'd moved perhaps a hundred yards through that blackness, Len whispered, "Wait." Standing motionless, I heard the sibilance of those crepe soles over cement. A doorknob squeaked faintly. As the door swung back, revealing him at the top of a short flight of cement steps, I blinked in a flood of fluorescent light. Taking the gun from its holster, he moved off into that glare. I followed.

Clean cement floor, contrasting with the

stone pillars that supported the vaulted roof. Against the far wall, a bank of dials. In the middle of the room, a huge metal cube—the central heating unit?—with big ducts sprouting from it to roof and sidewalls, like the arms of an octopus. Over in the far corner a generator, looking like an oversized metal barrel, throbbed steadily.

There was no one besides us in the room.

Len holstered the gun. "Come on."

I'd followed him for perhaps five steps when the earth suddenly shook, so hard that I staggered against the rock wall. Almost immediately there was a second, weaker shock. From somewhere in the vast structure above us, stone hurtled down upon stone, with a sound like distant thunder. White-faced, Len turned to me. "Come on. The power may go soon."

After a second I realized he must mean electric power. I didn't ask him, though, why it was important to us. I just followed him the rest of the way across the room, through a door, and up a flight of cement steps. At the top, Len opened another door.

Stone and stainless steel, ancient brick and modern porcelain, dimly lighted by a neon strip set into the stone wall above a huge and many-doored steel range. The kitchen.

I became aware of running feet in the cobblestoned courtyard outside, and a babble of voices—male and female, some angry, some high and thin with terror. A woman was screaming, "My daughter! I want to go to my daughter!"

"No one gets out!" It was Kurt's voice, raised to a bellow. "You're safer here. Can't you see that, you *Dummkopfs?*"

A man shouted, "Unlock that gate! Give me those keys, damn you, give me those—"

A shot. Momentarily a stunned silence, and then again that confused babble of terrified and furious voices.

Len said curtly, "Into the fireplace. As far as you can go. Wait there."

"The—the boys?"

"I'll get them and bring them here."

"Here! Why—"

"To take them with us. Don't you want that?" When I just stared at him, he added, "We're going into the tunnel, if the power stays on long enough. We'll be safer there, in every way. The mesa's solid granite. Even if this whole pile collapses, the mesa won't." He turned me around by the shoulders, gave me a little shove. "Go."

With a fleeting side glance toward the steel

panel set in the kitchen's southern wall, I hurried toward that shadowy cave where once Josiah Ward of Boston had run his palms futilely over dusty brick. Not stopping, I passed beneath its mantel of blackened oak. Here on either side were the stone benches Len had mentioned. Ahead, its opening both narrower and lower, was the hearth where once the actual cooking had been done. Even though the neon strip above Max Hind's huge range was at least fifty feet behind me, I could see the ancient spit extended between two iron uprights. I huddled beside it, on a stone floor long since swept clean of ashes.

From there I had almost a full view of the kitchen. It was empty now. Was Len, visored cap pulled low, pushing through that agitated crowd in the courtyard? Probably it would be safe to do so. Except for Kurt—and Ernesto too, if he was standing guard at the locked gates—surely no one would stop him, or even realize the clothes he wore were not his. Just the same, I decided, he'd probably taken the longer way around, through the western corridor to the stairs leading to the boys' room.

Did we have any right to take them with us? I couldn't be certain. But if Len's judgment was correct, if the tunnel was indeed safer, then surely we should take them.

Them. What if Len found only one terrified little boy in that room? But I wouldn't think about that.

Again the castle and the earth beneath it trembled. Out in the courtyard women screamed piercingly, and somewhere more stones quarried from the mesa nearly a thousand years ago thundered down. Yes, I thought, tightening my arms around my updrawn knees, we'd take them with us.

A door beside that huge steel range opened. With a canteen slung over his shoulder, and a boy's hand held in each of his, Len hurried toward the fireplace. I let out a kind of joyful whimper. Then they were with me in the little stone-floored cave. Tommy plastered damp kisses on one side of my face. Steven caught me around the neck in a strangling bear hug.

Crouched in the hearth opening, Len took the canteen and placed it beside me. "And keep this," he said, laying a long flashlight in my lap. "It's a spare. I got it out of my car." Reaching into a pocket of the baggy trousers, he brought out three small cardboard boxes. "Extra flashlight batteries. Put them in your skirt pocket."

As I obeyed he added, "I'll be back as soon as I can."

"Len! Where—?"

"I'm going to try to get that shortwave set."

"From Max Hind's—? You can't! He'll have someone up there with him. You'll get caught, maybe shot—"

"Honey, part of that observatory roof has collapsed." He gave a ghost of a grin. "Shoddy new construction. Not like they built in the old days. If the shortwave set isn't buried under concrete, maybe I can get it. Down in the tunnel, it'll be the only way we'll have of knowing what's happening. Now just sit tight, all of you."

Anxiously I watched him stand up, walk from the fireplace, and then, turning right, disappear. Evidently he planned to retrace our route through the power plant and the vaults.

"Don't worry," Tommy said. "He'll get it."

I looked from him to Steven. The small faces were not only unafraid. They were happy. Now that they were with Len and me, nothing bad could happen. I became aware of what a terrible burden a child's faith can be.

Steven said, "I meant to get that man's gun, but I was afraid he'd wake up. He almost woke up when I took his keys."

With my stomach contracting, I said hastily, "You did fine."

"That tunnel we're going into. Is it the same one that was in that book?"

"Yes."

"Are we going through it clear to the bottom of the mesa?"

Was Len considering that? Perhaps. But probably, like me, he wasn't looking that far ahead, not in this strange and murky world where thick walls and solid earth shook.

They shook just then.

"I don't know, dear," I said hurriedly, through the renewed screaming in the courtyard. "And you mustn't mind these . . . earth tremors, or the way some people are so . . . excited. Things will be the same as always soon."

Of course they would be. Else—

We were silent for a while after that. Once we heard a shot. (It was the guard firing over people's heads, I explained swiftly, to try to make them go quietly to their rooms.) Once a stout woman rushed into the kitchen, inexplicably turned water on in one of the sinks set at right angles to the big range, turned it off again, and rushed out.

Only minutes later, we saw Len moving into the fireplace, bent with the burden he carried.

31

HE PLACED THE shortwave set on the floor outside the hearth opening and then, bending low, came in to sit beside us. He breathed raggedly.

Tommy said, "I told you he'd get it."

After perhaps a minute more of hard breathing, Len said, "It was easy. Those big doors were wide open. Looks as if somebody who had a key—Miss Walmsey, maybe—rushed in after part of the dome collapsed, and then ran out, not bothering even to close the doors. It's a mess up there. That big telescope fell. You can see bits of it sticking up through the hunks of cement."

I said, "Max Hind?"

"Maybe under the cement. Maybe safe in his rooms. Maybe out there among that mob in the courtyard. Who knows?"

From his shirt pocket he took four candy bars. I recognized their blue-and-silver wrappings. When I was at school in England, those six-ounce chocolate bars had been my favorite form of dissipation. "Tommy, you'll be in charge of these. I got them from the supply room next to the kitchen. I wanted to look for food concentrates, but I was afraid to take the time. Steven, you carry the canteen. Put the strap over your shoulder. That's right. Dinah, keep the flashlight. All right. Let's go."

Swiftly we moved out of the fireplace, and across the shadowy kitchen to those electric ovens set in their panel of stainless steel. Hearing the continued clamor of the crowd in the courtyard, I had little fear that Kurt or anyone else guarding the gates would come in and try to stop us. Obviously they already had their hands full.

Len placed the shortwave set on the floor. After opening the door of the center oven, he took a thin steel file with an even-thinner curved end from his hip pocket. I heard a metallic rasp as the oven's false rear wall gave way. He must have touched the switch, because a three-foot-wide section of steel paneling swung silently on its axis and came to rest, with half of it projecting into the kitchen.

"You and the kids go ahead."

Steven went first through the opening. I followed, holding Tommy with one hand and the unlit flashlight with the other. A flight of cement steps led down into darkness. We descended a few steps, turned. Almost immediately Len appeared, carrying the shortwave set. He moved past us to the blackness below. I heard a grating sound as he lowered the set to some hard surface. Then he was back beside us.

"Dinah, shine the flashlight on the right-hand wall. See those switches? Put your finger on the one nearest the doorway, but don't press until I tell you to. All right. Now shine the flashlight down at the right-hand corner of the doorsill." Crouching, he placed the file upright in the angle between the sill and the doorjamb. "All right, press."

The panel swung toward its closed position until its edge met the obstructing file. Between the panel's edge and the jamb, a fraction of an inch of space was left. "If the power goes," he explained, "we'd have trouble getting out of here. This way, I'll be able to force the panel open."

"But if Kurt or someone noticed that crack in the paneling—"

"I know. We just have to weigh the

chances." He paused. "Shine the flashlight on those switches again."

He touched the second switch. Light sprang up the stairwell. I turned. A big ceiling globe, set in a wire cage, shed glare upon a section of the tunnel's cement wall, and upon the shortwave set resting on the clean cement floor. I said, puzzled, "Lights? After all these years?"

"Why not? They're obviously hooked into the circuits Max Hind's workmen left in place, just as the wall ovens are. And a light globe will last indefinitely, even in a socket, if it isn't corroded by salt air."

Switching off the flashlight, I followed Len and the boys down the steps. A glance to my left showed me that the tunnel ran only about thirty feet in that direction, ending in a cement wall. "The old fireplace entrance must have been somewhere along there," Len said.

With him in the lead, we turned in the other direction. When we'd gone only a few yards, he halted. Off to the right was a doorless little room that looked to be perfectly square. Against all three of its walls, flat packing cases of various sizes had been neatly stacked.

Len and I looked at each other. He nodded. The paintings. Those stolen pictures which had drawn both Len and Paul Duvall here, and which, indirectly, had brought death to a young girl. Len's face, not in the least triumphant, told me that he too was thinking of Juanita. "Come on," he said abruptly.

Under the glare of a second wire-caged light bulb, we moved on down the corridor, and then halted before the entrance to another side room. A swivel chair of plastic-upholstered metal, drawn up to a metal table. And on the table, a shortwave set. Moving quickly to it, Len turned the switch.

Silence. "Kaput," Len said. "Good thing we brought our own." He looked up. Following his gaze I saw a round hole about eight inches in diameter in the cement ceiling.

He climbed onto the table, thrust his hand into the opening. From the motion of his wrist and arm I knew he was turning something his hand had encountered.

Getting down from the table, he said, "The cap should be up now."

"Cap?"

"That's the opening of a ventilation pipe you see up there. It sticks about a foot and a half above the ground, and has a metal cap on it. I found four, strung out along the mesa. Each one was concealed by junipers and low bushes. Our Nazi friends, after they'd enlarged part of the old tunnel, put in those pipes and then did a little landscape gardening around them."

"I found two pipes," Tommy said. "One of them hurt me."

"Well, this one's going to help us. Whoever operated this old set must have threaded the antenna up through the pipe. I can do the same. If the antenna on the other set isn't long enough to reach above the ground, I'll use the antenna from this one."

Lifting the useless set from the table, he lowered it to the floor. "Back in a minute," he said, and left us.

The boys and I sat down, backs against the wall. I put an arm around each of them, and Tommy, with a little sigh, rested his head against my shoulder.

Never in my life had I dreamed that I, who hated even to go down into a cellar, would feel safe and almost happy in a concrete tunnel slanting down through the earth.

32

STAGGERING UNDER THE weight of the short-wave set, Len returned to the little room. With an expelled breath of relief, he placed it on the table, and began to extend its collapsed antenna upward. Its tip disappeared through the hole in the ceiling. Still he threaded sections of the steel rod upward. At last he said, "That ought to do it. The tip ought to be four or five feet above the—"

Through the wall at my back, and the floor on which I sat, came a rippling shock, almost as if the cement and the solid rock beneath it had been transformed into tar, or some other viscous substance. Even down here, the tremor had felt as severe as the one which had destroyed the northwest tower's concrete dome. I looked at Len, who'd turned away from the set. His face was white.

Abruptly he turned back, sat down on the swivel chair, and flipped the set on.

"—estimate that disturbances will reach their maximum within the next hour," a voice said in French. The words came through a steady crackling sound. "All persons are urged to maintain calm, and to obey orders of police and military personnel as quickly as possible. This ends the report from the Royal Observatory at Edinburgh.

"The report from the Ministry of the Interior reads as follows: All bridges spanning the Seine are now under water. It is hoped that sandbags previously placed to protect the Louvre, the Chamber of Deputies, the Cathedral of Notre Dame, and other historic buildings will keep damage to a minimum. As for seacoast cities, the naval base at Toulon reports all major installations under water—"

Len turned the dial. "—south bank of Thames completely evacuated to a depth of two miles." Incredibly, BBC's voice held a slight tremor. "Her Majesty's Ministry for Air reports that all army and navy aircraft have been flown to inland bases at Salis—"

Another shock came, jolting Len's chair so that he had to grip the metal table. The lights went out. Tommy whimpered, and my arms tightened around both boys.

The voice of BBC faded, then swelled, then faded again. "Turn on the flashlight," Len said.

I did, and laid it beside me on the floor. By its refracted glow, I saw Len spin the dial, turn up the volume. Weak, interspersed with crackles and high-pitched squeals, the American voice came, sounding as far away as if on another planet.

"—based in Norfolk, San Diego, San Francisco, Pearl Harbor, and all other naval bases have put out to sea to ride out the disturbances.

"Evacuation of low-lying areas on all coasts is almost complete. Manhattan Island as far north as—"

Another shock set the flashlight in motion. On the opposite wall, its circle of light rolled like a hoop. The faint voice abruptly ceased.

Len twirled the dial. Only crackles, and that shrill squealing. He kept on trying for perhaps five interminable minutes. Then he sat motionless. "Well," he said finally, not turning around, "That's that. Too much interference."

Of course. That's why those voices all over the world no longer spoke to us. Because of that electromagnetism Len had mentioned, broadcasting was now impossible. It would be silly to torment one's self by conjuring up some other explanation.

Len walked over and picked up the flashlight. I asked, "What time is it?"

He glanced at his watch. "Four minutes after two."

"Morning, or—?" Somehow I'd lost track.

"Morning."

Tommy said, "I'm hungry." He didn't add, "And I'm frightened," but his tone did. Steven said nothing, just sat ramrod straight in the half circle of my arm.

We broke one of those big chocolate bars into four roughly equal pieces, and followed the meal with two swallows of water each from the canteen. "We'd better save the flashlight battery, even if we do have spares," Len said. "Besides, we'd better try to sleep. You take the chair."

"No, the boys couldn't lean against me then." I tried to put a smile into my voice. "And anyway, you're our leader. You should have the best sleeping place, for all our sakes."

He didn't argue. The chair creaked as he sat down. Tommy stretched out with his head in my lap. Steven leaned against my left shoulder. Len turned the flashlight off. Hearing a metallic click, I knew he'd laid it on the table beside the silent shortwave set.

I stared into the utter blackness, and was sure Len did the same. Don't think. Don't even think about what might have happened

298

to that ancient structure on the mesa's surface, let alone all over—

Sleep.

Impossible to sleep. I thought, aware of a dangerous interior welling of laughter, "McGrath hath murdered sleep."

Stop that. You've got two children on your hands. *Close your eyes.*

33

SOMEWHERE A VOICE shouted, and fists hammered against metal. I thought, "So I must have slept, after all," and opened my eyes onto utter blackness.

The pounding and shouting went on. Len's voice. I listened, willing myself not to speculate about what it meant. The exhausted children slept on, Steven against my shoulder, Tommy curled up with his head resting on my now stiff and aching thighs.

The racket ceased. A path of bobbing light cut through the tunnel's blackness. For an instant before he switched off the flashlight, I saw his figure looming in the doorway.

His footsteps approached me. "Dinah?"

"I'm awake. The boys aren't."

He must have crouched, because when he

next spoke his voice seemed to come from a point on a level with my head. "We're going to have to go the rest of the way through the tunnel."

I said, through a sudden, high-pitched ringing in my ears, "You mean that the panel we came through—?"

"One of those heavy jolts last night dislodged the file. The panel's locked, locked solid, and with the power gone there's no way of opening it. I ran against it, but I'm sure I could do that until my shoulder was a pulp, and it would still hold."

"You were shouting—"

"Yes. Either that slab of steel is too thick, or everyone's away from the kitchen area."

"Yes," I said quickly, not letting my thoughts shape any other possibilities. "All right, I don't like tunnels, but this one doesn't seem so bad. We haven't heard any cement falling or—"

"Dinah, give me your hands."

I extended them into the blackness and his hands closed around them. "Listen, darling. Those men thirty years ago enlarged the tunnel for only a few yards more. I'm not sure why they enlarged it even to that extent, but maybe they planned to store more loot down here. Anyway, we'll have to

go the rest of the way through the old tunnel."

The old tunnel. Men long dead, laden
with crossbows, and bodies bent double as
they hurried through a rough-walled, slanting tube to surprise besiegers on the
plain . . .

"Dinah! Your hands are like ice. I know
it will be tough. But we've got to do it. We
can't stay here until that little bit of food and
water is gone, and then just—"

"Then there's no point in arguing about
it, is there?"

I'd do it. I'd do it because I had to. And
if I went off my head in there—well, maybe Len could knock me out and drag me the
rest of the way.

"No, no point in arguing. In fact, we're
lucky. They'd started to cement up the
entrance to what's left of the old tunnel. Why
they didn't finish the job, we'll probably
never know. Maybe the war ended, and
they decided to make tracks. Anyway, if they
had closed it off . . ."

"Turn on the light," I said swiftly. "I'll
wake up the boys."

I shook Steven awake, and then Tommy.
Small faces white with fatigue, eyes blinking

in the flashlight's glare, they reminded me of two disturbed owls.

Tommy said, "Where—" and then broke off.

"We're still in the tunnel, all nice and safe." Would it fool even a one-year-old, that bright, bright voice? "We're going to eat some chocolate, and then we're going to have an adventure. Remember my telling you about sieges? Well, we're going to do what people in the castle used to do long, long ago when it was under siege. We're going through the tunnel, and when we come out, we'll be down on the plain."

"I'm glad," Tommy said. "I don't like it here." Steven, blue eyes regarding me steadily, said nothing.

A sudden question formed in my mind. For several seconds I stopped breathing. Too bad I hadn't thought of it before I woke the boys. But now that I had thought of it, I'd have to ask it, I'd have to.

I stretched my lips into an incongruous smile. "What if we find the tunnel blocked at one point or another?"

His smile too was a parody. "Then we'll unblock it. I've got that file to work with."

That file, that thin little file. "What time is it?"

"Eight-fifteen."

"In the morning?"

"Yes. We couldn't have slept more than five or six hours."

We had breakfast—another of those chocolate bars. I found it hard to swallow. Even after I'd taken two mouthfuls of water, my throat felt sticky.

With Len in the lead—the flashlight in his hand, the canteen slung over his shoulder, the file projecting from his hip pocket —we left the little room and walked perhaps forty feet. Halting, Len played the flashlight's beam over a jagged face of granite. The old tunnel's opening, its lower edge about two feet above the cement floor upon which we stood, was roughly oval-shaped and slightly flattened at the bottom. It measured perhaps three feet at its widest point, almost four feet at its highest. Glancing to the left side of the granite face, I saw a neat, foot-wide strip of cement. I was glad it was there. The shuddering thought of what would have become of us if they'd completed that cement job seemed to lend me courage for the journey ahead.

"You three mind waiting in the dark for a minute or two?" Len asked. "I want to check the shortwave."

Turning, he followed the flashlight's beam back to the little side room. We stood watching the faint glow shine out into the tunnel. After a moment the set made crackling noises, interspersed with those shrill whistles.

The sound persisted for perhaps three minutes. Then he came walking back to us. I tried to speak offhandedly. "Well?"

"Still too much static. I could hear voices, but I couldn't make out the words."

He'd moved past me toward the opening of the tunnel as he spoke. Was he lying? Of course he isn't, I told myself sternly. Of course he'd heard voices.

Turning, he said, "I'll go first, then Steven, then Tommy, then you." In the flashlight's refracted glow his face looked strained and thin, the cheekbones more prominent than they'd been only a few days before. "All set?"

I nodded. "We'll—go fast?"

"As fast as we can."

With a strangely adult gesture, Steven grabbed my hand and squeezed it. "We'll run."

Len climbed into the old tunnel's mouth and then, crouching, turned to grasp Steven's hands and draw him inside. Next he

304

lifted Tommy in. Finally he helped me in. "Keep watching your head," he told me.

I didn't answer. Head and shoulders bent beneath the jagged low roof, I watched the others turn—the boys erect, Len bent from the waist—and move away. I drew several deep breaths, and then followed along the downward-sloping passage. Sharp edges of rock bit through the soles of my sneakers. Now and then, losing my balance, I bruised an arm or a shoulder against the sidewall. That didn't matter. All that mattered was trying not to think of the roof inches above my bent head and back, or of how deep in the mesa we must be by now, or of how much farther we had to go.

I kept my eyes on Tommy's small form, outlined by the flashlight's glow, as he trotted forward. Once his feet slipped out from under him, but before I could reach him he scrambled up and, without a word, trotted on.

How far had we gone? A third of the way? Half? Oh, surely at least a third. But I really had no way of telling, not when I didn't know how long the tunnel was.

How far away had the mesa's western edge appeared to be when I looked at it from that second floor window in the castle? No, don't think of the mesa. That hundred feet or more of solid granite separating me from the surface of the earth . . .

Down here the granite sometimes gleamed with pinpoints of color—brown, white, green, red, as the light touched it. It must be bits of various minerals reflecting the glow. Think about that. Try to remember what granite is made of. "Granite is an igneous rock, composed typically of quartz, mica, feldspar—" Feldspar, or something else?

I found it increasingly hard to breathe. Could it be that the air was—? Of course not. Bands, perhaps large bands, of armed men had hurried single file along this tunnel in the past. If the air had been sufficient for them, surely it should be for two adults and two children.

Unless, of course, there'd been some sort of crude ventilation system centuries ago. Shafts in the tunnel roof, now long since blocked by encroaching vegetation which had flourished and died, and been buried by soil, which in turn had nourished more vegetation, until no air possibly could move down into—

Len's voice, almost unrecognizable in that

confined space, came back to me. "At ease, gang. Take a break."

He'd halted. So had the boys. "No!" I cried before I could stop myself.

Carefully Len turned in that narrow passage. Above the boys' heads he looked at me. Haggard face, bent back. A thin young Atlas with the world on his shoulders.

He said, "Dinah, sit down. All three of you, sit down. There's a rock slide ahead. Must be a strata of sedimentary rock there. Maybe it came down last night. Anyway, there's this pile blocking the tunnel . . ."

His voice trailed off. Then he repeated, almost harshly, "Sit down."

I sat. So did the boys, with Tommy next to me. Thickening dark as Len moved away with the flashlight. Then a sliding sound. He must have dislodged a rock. Yes, and tossed it away. I heard it strike the tunnel floor.

How wide was the strata, and therefore the barrier of fallen rock? Three feet wide? Twenty? Thirty? I became aware that I breathed in shallow gasps. How low the tunnel roof seemed, in the faint light that filtered back to us. It should seem higher, now that I was sitting down. But instead it appeared to have descended. Even as I looked at it, it seemed to move a fraction of an inch closer—

Steven said, "Tommy, say the multiplication table." To me: "He made only three mistakes the other day."

"Two times two is four," Tommy began.

Oh, bless them, bless them. I listened as attentively as if my life, rather than just my sanity, depended upon it. The sounds from perhaps twenty feet away in the tunnel seemed to grow dim.

"—four times eight is twenty-three."

"Thirty-two." Still that sliding sound, and then the impact of a tossed stone against solid granite. Don't look that way. Stare at the wall opposite and listen to Tommy.

"Four times eight is thirty-two, four times nine is thirty-six—"

The high young voice continued its singsong. Len was using the chisel now. I could hear the rasp of metal against rock.

"—seven times nine is sixty-one—"

"Sixty-three."

"Seven times nine is sixty-three, seven times ten is seventy, seven times eleven is seventy-seven, seven times twelve is eighty-four, and that's as far as I know."

Slide. Impact of rock.

Steven said, "The major capitals of the

world are: United States of America, Washington, D.C., Republic of France, Paris; West Germany, Bonn; United Kingdom—"

Footsteps hurrying toward us. In the upward-striking light, Len's face glistened with sweat. "All right. We can get by."

We followed him, along a tunnel floor now strewn with the rocks he'd tossed away, stones rounded and smoothed by some stream that had stopped flowing perhaps a million years ago. When we reached the barrier, I saw that it still blocked most of the tunnel. He'd managed to clear a narrow space of perhaps a foot and a half, though, between the top of the rock pile and the tunnel's roof.

He handed me the flashlight. "I'll go first. Then boost the boys up, backward, and I'll pull them over."

Using both hands and feet, he wriggled his way over that unstable pile and through the opening. On the other side, rocks clattered to the tunnel floor as he slid downward, head first. After a moment he said, "All right. Hand Tommy over."

I did. Len's hands caught his hands and drew him through the opening. Steven went next.

Len called, "Give me the flashlight."

Leaning against the pile, I extended the flashlight through the opening. As he grasped it, I saw that his fingers, scraped raw, oozed blood.

"Here's the flashlight, Steven. All right, Dinah. Lean back against the pile and reach your hands up."

As he drew me over the stones, I felt wonder that neither of the boys, not even Tommy, had cried when the hard, sliding surfaces had pressed through his clothing. Catching me under the arms, Len drew me backward until my feet, slipping and sliding, descended to the tunnel floor.

He released me. "I think we're almost there. Would you like to rest?"

"No!" I started to straighten up but remembered in time not to. Head and shoulders bent, I turned. "Let's go on."

The slope grew steeper after that. Frequently I had to clutch at the rough wall to keep from falling. No matter. Soon . . .

A current of air. Surely it was a current of air, blowing my hair back from my damp forehead. Seconds later, I could have sobbed with disappointment. Len had halted and was playing the flashlight's beam over a sloping pile of rock-studded earth that appeared to block the whole passage.

"Last hurdle," he said. "I'm sure it's the last. I can feel air blowing in. Yes, up there at the top. See that little space?"

All of us worked at that earth barrier, Len and I enlarging with our hands and the file that narrow space at the top, and the boys throwing handfuls of dislodged earth and stones aside. When the space was big enough, Len wriggled through, and then drew the boys to the other side. I came through last, and found myself amid tangled bushes, their leaves gray-green in the murky light coming through the tunnel entrance.

We went through the bushes headlong, heedless of scratches and ripped clothing. Just beyond the tunnel's mouth was the juniper grove I'd noticed the day we drove up onto the mesa. We ran between the trees and out onto the plain.

Flat, arid earth, blessedly still underfoot, and a lowering sky. Not a gray sky. Faintly brownish. From dust? Probably. Through that brownish overcast the sun sent down a sullen, coppery glow. In the west, just above the horizon, a much smaller patch of coppery light showed through the dust-laden mist.

I knew it must be the little Scots boy's comet, outward bound at last upon its long, long journey.

Silent, moving slowly now, we walked about a hundred yards farther out onto the plain. Len stopped and looked back, and so did the boys and I. Up there on the mesa, all of the castle's round towers had vanished. The western wall seemed intact, except for great gaps in the crenelation.

How many were alive up there? Any at all?

Very slowly I turned and looked toward the west. The sun, breaking through a thinner portion of the overcast, awoke a diffused gleam at the plain's edge.

The Atlantic. Before visible only from the mesa, it now showed itself to us down here on the plain. How far had it advanced inland? Ten miles? More? And on other coasts, how far—?

I forced myself to turn and look at Len. He too was staring at that diffused gleam. His bleak profile told me, as clearly as if he'd spoken, that he had lied about hearing faint voices over the shortwave that morning.

Suddenly the stillness had a terrible quality.

As if feeling my gaze, he turned. In his eyes I saw the same questions that had taken form in my own mind.

A new Adam? A new Eve?

With Cain and Abel already beside us?

For several more seconds we stared at each other through that stillness. Then voices broke it. Unwilling to trust my own hearing, I stayed rigid for a moment.

When I turned, I saw a little procession moving around the mesa's sloping southern end, about a dozen men and women, and seven or eight children. The man in the lead held the halter of a donkey. Its rough coat gleamed like silver through the murky light. Several others, including a young boy, led goats. In the stillness, the bleating of the goats, and the voices of the men and women—dazed and hushed as human voices usually are in the aftermath of shock—came to us clearly.

Another sound. We looked up. In the north, ten small planes broke through the overcast. They flew directly overhead so low that we could see the government markings on their wings, and then continued south.

My throat aching with joy, I smiled at Len. He smiled back, not his usual quick grin, but a slow, spreading smile. Those planes meant much more than that ten men had survived to fly them. Other men, rang-ing from government officials to officers at the airfield, must have passed along the order that had sent those planes aloft. Still others had checked engines and runways, filled fuel tanks, and manned a control tower. Wives must have managed, despite quake-damaged walls and broken gas mains, to prepare some sort of breakfast for all those men, and children had kissed them goodbye.

If it was thus in this little corner of the world, why not almost everywhere? A sentence went through my mind: "And the earth abides."

Len took Steven's hand, and I took Tommy's, and we walked toward the little procession of adults and children and bleating goats.